Prairie Schooner Book Prize in Fiction   EDITOR   Kwame Dawes

When Are You Coming Home?

{ STORIES }

Bryn Chancellor

UNIVERSITY OF NEBRASKA PRESS   LINCOLN AND LONDON

Library of Congress Cataloging-in-Publication Data
Chancellor, Bryn.
[Short stories. Selections]
When are you coming home?:
stories / Bryn Chancellor.
pages   cm.—(Prairie Schooner Book Prize in fiction)
ISBN 978-0-8032-7722-9 (pbk.: alk. paper)
ISBN 978-0-8032-8476-0 (epub)
ISBN 978-0-8032-8477-7 (mobi)
ISBN 978-0-8032-8478-4 (pdf)
I. Title.
PS3603.H35595A6 2015
813'.6—dc23
2015013432

Set in Alda by M. Scheer.
Designed by N. Putens.

To my mother, Cathy, and my brother, Roy,
and in memory of my father, Alan

Night from a railroad car window

Is a great, dark, soft thing

Broken across with slashes of light.

—CARL SANDBURG, "Window"

CONTENTS

Acknowledgments ix

When Are You Coming Home? 1

Wrestling Night 18

Meet Me Here 31

Water at Midnight 44

Any Sign of Light 56

At the Terminal 69

All This History at Once 85

Fossil Light 91

This Is Not an Exit 108

I am grateful to the Arizona Commission on the Arts, Sewanee Writers' Conference, Bread Loaf Writers' Conference, and Vanderbilt University; their generous support has been instrumental in my growth as a writer. Thanks, too, to Poets & Writers and Maureen Egen for the Writers Exchange Award; to Victor LaValle for selecting my stories; and to Bonnie Marcus and Lynne Connor for their assistance and kindness. I also am indebted to the Alabama State Council on the Arts and to literary arts advocates Jeanie Thompson, Anne Kimzey, and Danny Gamble.

I owe so much to everyone involved in the Prairie Schooner Book Prize and to the University of Nebraska Press; thank you for choosing these stories and for publishing them. Thanks especially to the wonderful Kwame Dawes, Ashley Strosnider, Kristen Elias Rowley, Maggie Boyles, Joeth Zucco, and Mary M. Hill and to everyone who shepherded the manuscript.

To all the literary journals in which these stories first appeared—*Blackbird*, the *Colorado Review, Crazyhorse, descant, Gulf Coast, Phoebe*, PMS: *Poemmemoirstory*, and the *Yalobusha Review*—thanks for giving my work its first home. Special thanks to editors Stephanie G'Schwind, Anne Corbitt, and Matt Ellsworth, who made the work better.

I can never repay my debt to all my writing mentors and teachers at Vanderbilt and elsewhere: Lorraine López, Tony Earley, Nancy Reisman, Peter Guralnick, Ron Carlson, Maxine Clair, Pam Houston, Jill McCorkle, Bret Lott, and Ann Cummins. At Vanderbilt, thanks also to Margaret Quigley, Mark Jarman, Kate Daniels, Rick Hilles, Mark Schoenfield, Teresa Goddu, and Dana Nelson.

I am fortunate beyond measure to have so many remarkable friends, both writers and otherwise, whose support has buoyed me over the years. Boundless thanks to Joy Castro, Tayari Jones, Meredith K. Gray, Alex Moody, Casebeer, Toni Jensen, Matthew Pitt, and Kevin Wilson; to the Sewanee Side Huggers: Marjorie Sa'adah, Justin Quarry, Nina McConigley, David Roby, Derek Palacio, Nickole Brown, Jessica Jacobs, Amy Arthur, and Robie Jackson; to my pals in journalism, especially Jennifer Johnson, Mike Ambri, Jeff Gary, and Tom Travin; to my many colleagues and friends at the University of Montevallo and in the Birmingham area, especially Stephanie L. Batkie, Betsy Inglesby, and Steve Forrester, as well as the Faculty Workgroup, who helped me finish the final story in this collection.

To Missy Knutson Hart and Nicole Thompson Goring for all the love and adventures. To Brandon Nelson and Jorge Sánchez, excellent men for my best girls. To Tiffany Engelmann Wiley and Rick Wiley for the love, laughter, and all the Chico's. To Elizabeth Wetmore, who knows all my stories; my writing and, more importantly, my life are better because of you. And to my dearest Gina Dozeman Nelson: I would steal all the bees back for you. Thanks for believing in me all these long, lovely years.

To all my families: Roy, Robyn, Nathan, and Kelsey Chancellor; Diane and Wayne and the entire Winkler crew; the Cowans; the Dozemans; and the Skaggses. To my late father, Alan Chancellor, a wonder in life whose absence is still a living force; and to my mother, Cathy Chancellor Wright, who is brave, beautiful, and magnificent.

Finally, and forever, to Timothy Winkler: Home is wherever you are.

WHEN ARE YOU COMING HOME?

When Are You Coming Home?

Robert Cannon kept busy in his new part-time job as a locksmith. He'd spent thirty years running his own handyman business, everything from window repair to ceiling fan installation, plumbing and electrical to carpentry. He was quick and reliable, and his boss—a man half his age who wouldn't know a pin-tumbler lock if it hit him in the face—called on him often. In this new city, Cannon drove the unfamiliar neighborhoods with a map open on the seat next to him while his wife took swim lessons down at the Y. People were always moving, landlords switching the locks for the next tenant, and the jobs blurred into one another: empty rooms, vinyl blinds with slats missing, the odors of cigarettes and cat urine in the carpet submerged by the fumes of cheap paint. Remove knob, pop out cylinder plug and rearrange pins, pop it back, reattach knob. In and out, easy-peasy, a tidy paycheck to flesh out the savings. That was fine. He didn't need the money so much as he needed to keep busy.

His boss called early that morning. We got a live one for you. Lady's all upset. Right-o, let's get on over there, pronto. At home,

Cannon sometimes made a joke of his boss's strange patter: Right-o, buck-o, let's get that dinner out pronto, he'd say to Jenny, and sometimes she'd smile before she caught herself. The job was in an older neighborhood in central Phoenix, not far from where he and Jenny had rented a little condo off Central Avenue, their own house up north in Flagstaff locked up tight, the phone disconnected, the utility bills forwarded, Jenny's piano covered with a sheet. Cannon had taped a small Out of Business sign in the window of his shop.

The job was on a street called Heatherbrae. Cannon said the name aloud, liking the airy sound of it. He pulled up to the curb and left the engine idling with the AC on low as he gathered his paperwork. Though it was only March, the days down here were already well into the eighties, thin blue skies and sunshine that burned his pale skin through the truck windows. He rummaged in the glove box for the tube of sunscreen he'd put in there. His hand fell on a plastic baggie of keys, spares he'd kept from earlier jobs. He held them up to the light for a moment before he tucked them away.

In the Heatherbrae yard, a cardboard sign stuck on two sticks and plugged into the grass read YARD SALE. EVERYTHING *MUST* GO! Several blankets stretched across the browned-out Bermuda grass. On the blankets were heaps of clothing, mismatched dinner plates, a food processor, an old rotary phone. Dangling from a branch of a small olive tree was a wedding dress. As Cannon got out of his truck, a woman stepped from the doorway and flung an armful of what appeared to be men's flannel shirts onto a blanket. The woman stood next to the blanket with her hands on her hips. She'd been crying, he could tell, her face blotchy red. She was young, maybe late twenties, with brown hair that corked off her head in tight curls. About Felice's age, perhaps a bit older.

She looked at Cannon. "I'm not ready yet. Come back later."

"Ma'am." Cannon held up his hands. He pointed at the magnetic sign on the door of his truck. "I'm here for the locks."

She stared at him a moment and then nodded. "Oh. Right. There's only two doors, front and back. I'll show you." She waved him to follow her. He stepped over the edge of a blanket, over an old manual typewriter and a box of books. He caught a title, *Serpent-Handling Believers*.

The house was a small postwar brick ranch, with low ceilings, plaster walls, a great room with painted concrete floors, and casement windows with the cranks missing. Inside, a little girl sat on a giant yellow pillow on the floor in front of the television. Cartoon noises echoed in the sparsely furnished room.

"Gigi, turn that down. Good grief." The girl kept staring at the cartoon characters on the screen. The woman picked the remote off the coffee table and turned the volume down. "I don't usually let her watch TV. Look at her. It's like crack." She ruffled the girl's hair and dropped a kiss on her forehead. The girl kept her eyes on the screen. The child was about Cannon's granddaughter's age, six or seven. Cannon had seen his grandchildren only twice in four months, since his daughter-in-law's funeral. His son's burial. The other grandparents had custody, of course, no question there. No question.

The woman said, "I lost my purse. Left it right in the shopping cart." She thumped her forehead with the heel of her hand. "My license has my address on it. It's probably overkill, but better to be safe, right? There's the back door there. Can I get you something to drink?"

Her hair was a bit of a wonder, actually. He had the urge to pull on a curl, to watch it spring back. "No, ma'am. I'm fine. I have water in the truck."

"I'm Kyla," she said. "Holler if you need anything. I'll be in and out."

"Bob," he said, though he'd been Robert his entire life. "Thank you."

He set his toolbox near the back door and pulled a new set of keys from his bag of tricks, as Jenny called it. He pictured her down at the Y, in her swim cap and goggles, which left deep indents around her nose and eyes and hairline. She had never learned to swim and had always been terrified of the water. When they moved down from the cool pines of Flagstaff to the desert of Phoenix, with all its flashing backyard pools, she'd decided to give it a try. What else am I going to do? she said. I mean, really, what? She took private lessons with a young man who competed in triathlons, his arms and seemingly hairless chest lean and roped with muscles. Jenny practiced floating on her back or lying face down in three feet of water. Prostrate, she clawed and clenched at the young man's hands as if she were sliding off a cliff. She'd flail upward, gasping, until her feet touched bottom. At home, in the condo's heated community pool, she'd get a death grip on the tile gutter and practice putting her face in the water, blowing bubbles, her silver hair poking out from the edges of her cap. Every time, she jerked up for air as if someone were trying to hold her down. Cannon could swim fine, and he offered to help her practice, but she didn't want his help. At the pool, he sat on the vinyl patio furniture in the shade with the newspaper unread on his lap. The smell of orange blossoms and cut grass hung like fog in the air. He obsessively rubbed sunscreen along his pale neck and into the deep wrinkles on the tops of his hands.

He had the back door knob off when he noticed the little girl, Gigi, standing next to him. She hopped on one foot and the other. Her hair was cut as short as a boy's, but he could see her mother's curl in it, little swirls along her scalp. The shortness of the bangs suggested she'd gotten hold of the scissors, and the short cut was a fix-up job.

"Can I help?" she said. "Daddy lets me help. I'm a *really* good helper."

Cannon picked up two screws he'd set aside. "You can hold these for me." She grinned and held out cupped hands. Cannon's hand trembled as he set the screws in her palms. He put the cylinder plug back together, popped it back in its slot, and tested the new key.

"Looks good." He held his hand out. Gigi, the tip of her tongue taut against her upper lip, poured the screws from her hands as if the screws were precious gems.

"You're a good apprentice," he told her.

"I know." She nodded, eyes wide.

"Let's do the other one, then." He picked up his tools and headed to the front door. Gigi trailed behind him, jumping from foot to foot as if doing hopscotch. His grandchildren did that, too. He balled his hands, willing them to be steady.

"Daddy and Judy have a cat. His name is Mr. Cat. Do you have a cat?"

Cannon shook his head. He knelt in front of the door, and just then Kyla came bursting through it. The knob hit him in the throat, taking his wind, and he fell onto his backside.

"Oh, God. Oh!" Kyla bent over him, her hand at her mouth. "Are you all right?"

Gigi ran toward the kitchen. "I'll call the police! 9-1-1! 9-1-1!"

"No, please. I'm fine." He coughed. "I'm fine."

"Gigi, stop. Put the phone away. It's all right."

Kyla held out her hand, but he ignored it. He grunted and struggled upright. As he stood, a wave of dizziness hit him, and he slumped against the wall.

Kyla reached up under him. He gave in and rested some weight on her shoulders. She smelled of sweet shampoo, green apples or some kind of berry. She said, "I'm so sorry. I'm such an idiot." She led him to the sofa and then got him a glass of ice water. He sipped at it, touching his tender throat.

In the corner of the room, Gigi dug around in a set of toy bins.

He said, "It's good she knows to call for help. These days."

Kyla glanced at Gigi. "Her father taught her that." She gave a short laugh and nodded at the room. "I'm getting ready to sell this place. I'm done with memories. Time to move on."

Gigi carried a toy first-aid kit and a doll. She held out the doll to Cannon. "That's Florence. You can hold her if you want."

Cannon took the doll. It had matted red curls and was missing a button eye. Gigi opened her kit and held up a roll of white gauze. She hopped up on the sofa next to him.

Kyla said, "Gigi."

"It's all right," Cannon said. The ice in his glass rattled as he set the glass on a coaster. Gigi started to wind the gauze around his head. She dropped the roll, and it unraveled down his arm and to the floor. Gigi breathed on his neck and kept winding the gauze. Chill-bumps rose on his arms.

Cannon watched the ceiling fan spin. It was a little off balance. He spotted a crack in the plaster near a window. He said, "I do repair work. If you need help with the house. I'm retired technically, but I do it on the side for a little extra." He hadn't meant to say it. He hadn't done anything but locks at all down here, but that didn't mean he couldn't. He pulled an old business card from his wallet, scratched out the number, and put his new cell phone number down. He handed it to her, holding his breath as she looked at it. Would she recognize the name and connect it to headlines? Such news had a way of traveling.

But Kyla smiled and put the card in her shirt pocket. "That's very nice of you. I probably will take you up on that. I promise not to knock you off a ladder or anything."

He smiled back. Gigi bandaged his hands, loose coils between each finger.

"I'll take care of you," the girl said.

*

When Cannon got home from work, Jenny was in the pool, which was in the center of the U-shaped condo units. He saw her shiny purple swim cap as he pulled into the covered parking space. She didn't look up as he approached. She held tight to the wall, blowing bubbles and jerking her head up for a breath every three seconds or so.

"Jenny." He leaned down and tapped her head, and she let out a garbled scream, flailing upright.

"Good Christ. You scared me." Her eyes were unreadable behind the tinted goggles. She flexed her hands on the wall. They were white and shriveled at the tips from the water and chlorine. "You're home early."

He said, "It's late. You're pruned up. I think your back's burned. Come inside."

He expected her to argue, their standard exchange lately. Instead she waded to the steps, climbed out, and toweled off. She'd lost weight from her already small frame. The suit gapped at the top and sagged around her legs. She snapped off her cap and goggles. Dark red indents marked her eyes and nose.

"I'll lotion your back," he said.

"I'm fine," she said.

Inside the condo, Jenny set to work making supper, still in her short toweling robe over her damp swimsuit. All the tile made the place sound empty, though it came furnished. Cannon missed the sound of Jenny's piano, her flawless posture, the way her long fingers seemed to float over the keys. Cannon set the table and watched her tense, sloped back as she moved in the short space between stove and sink and refrigerator. After thirty-five years, he knew how she moved. He knew a pressure was building in her. She hated confrontation, avoided it until the emotions she had tamped down erupted, forced out like flames from a ruptured gas pipe. In those hot moments, he'd seen her tip over sofas, break whole sets of wine glasses, and bash in the hood of a car, though she never struck him or their son. She'd gotten better over the years, learning to talk it out, keeping it more of a controlled burn than an explosion. But Robert Jr. never had learned. Cannon had seen it in him as they worked together in those last weeks, saw it in the tight hunch of his son's back as he turned wrenches and hammered nails and changed air filters. There was a flat edge in his son's voice when he called Felice: That's not what I meant. Don't put words in my mouth. Who's going with you? It's just a question. It's *just* a question. After a call, he sat slumped and pale in the passenger seat of the truck. Tamping it down. No sense in prodding him, Cannon had thought. He'd talk when he was ready. But he didn't.

Cannon looked down at his hands. His son's hands had been exact replicas, down to the long nail beds and thick knuckles.

"Jenny," he said.

"Don't pick at me right now, Robert," she said. "Leave it be, all right?"

"I'm not picking," he said. "I was going to tell you about my day."

"No you weren't."

"So now you can read my mind?"

"Here we go," she said.

He looked at his palms. Working hands. Rough hands.

"He had your temper," he said to his wife.

Jenny didn't answer. She picked up the pot of peas she'd set to boil on the stove and turned them onto the floor. They steamed in a green pile on the ceramic tile, the water spreading into the channels of grout. She stepped over the pile and hurried to the bedroom, her plastic shoes smacking the tile. He got a whiff of chlorine. He could hear the bathwater running. Soon, she would be in the tub, making herself float facedown in the shallow water. Breathing, breathing. It grew dark as Cannon sat at the table. Finally, he got up and headed to his truck.

The moon shone bright through the thin branches of the paloverdes and jacarandas lining the driveway, and he gazed up at it for a long moment. The city's light pollution, though, dulled the stars. Back home, constellations and planets burned diamond-white against a velvet sky. As he backed out of the drive, he pulled the baggie of keys from the glove box and set them on the seat. He hadn't started out keeping them. One afternoon, he'd found an extra set in his shirt pocket from that morning's job, a little brick house for rent on Osborn Road. He'd gone back to hand over the set, but the landlord was long gone. He'd put the key in the lock, an absentminded test, but when the door unlatched, he stepped inside the empty space, shutting the door behind him. He walked through the rooms again, the carpet soft under his boots. He noted a crack in the plaster ceiling. He flipped lights on and off, knocked on walls, straightened a blind in the master bedroom. He turned on the faucet and let it run, hand-tightened the P-trap nut under the kitchen sink. After ten minutes, he locked the door and went back to his truck, back to his regular day. Now, in the evenings when he couldn't sleep, or like tonight, he checked on these places that he knew by street names: Osborn, Montecito, Glenrosa, Indianola. Sometimes he simply drove by, and sometimes he went in, wandering the dark rooms, listening to the creaks in the silence. Nothing nefarious. He had no intentions. He just had an urge to check on things, these homes that did not belong to him.

The rental house on Osborn was still empty. He parked in the driveway and let himself in the front door, calling out a hello just in case. No one answered. The electricity was off, so he walked through the dark hall, running his hand along the drywall. In the back bedroom, he opened the closet where the breaker box was. He stood there, trying to decipher the labels on the panel, wishing he'd brought his flashlight. He rattled a clump of wire hangers.

He never said it aloud. In Flagstaff, where he'd lived for his entire fifty-four years, he'd never had to. Everyone knew. They knew Robert Cannon and his family: wife Jenny, son Robert Jr., daughter-in-law Felice (freckle-faced Felice, whom Cannon nicknamed Dots), two young grandchildren. Cannon had met Jenny at the university back when she had brown straight hair down to her waist and gave piano lessons to help pay for tuition. Jenny taught music at the high school for twenty-eight years.

Cannon built her a house, a wood and stone split-level off Lake Mary Road, the same road he'd grown up on, where they hiked, biked, and in winter cross-country skied in the woods behind the property. Cannon was the do-it-all handyman, owner of his own business, Cannon and Son—trustworthy, fast, affordable, like it said on their cards. He'd coached soccer and Little League, and Robert Jr. had too. They went to Lowell Observatory on summer nights, stood in the cold, pine-scented air and gaped through the telescopes at the moon's wavy craters, at comets and planets and other fuzzy celestial objects. They traveled to nearby destinations and once to Europe, for his and Jenny's twenty-fifth anniversary, and they would do more when they retired. That was how he believed he was known, how he wished to be known, how he knew himself. That life was bountiful beyond what he could have ever imagined. But now. Now. Everyone knew a different version. They all knew what he could not say aloud.

Cannon moved his hands in the dark, empty space of the closet, a movement that he imagined both sleeping and waking. He could not stop seeing it, or the results. Thumbprint bruises on a freckled neck. The scald of gunpowder on a face. He thrust his arms forward, then back, then up, banging his elbow on the closet door.

Her temper. His hands.

*

A week later, Kyla called Cannon and asked if he could repair windows. She had a few cracked panes in the casements. He could. He certainly could. After he finished with locks in the early afternoon, he called Jenny and left a message that he'd be home late and not to hold dinner. She didn't call back. He headed to the house on Heatherbrae.

Kyla was in the kitchen when he arrived. She wore a blue kerchief over her curls and denim overalls with a smear of white paint on the bib. "Kitchen trim," she said. She grinned and held up a pint of paint. She showed him the windows, and Gigi left her post in front of the television to follow him as he made measurements. The child, who wore a headband with a pair of glittery shamrocks bobbing on springs, chattered about Mr. Cat and a loose tooth. When he returned from the hardware store with cut panes, Gigi brought him a plastic tumbler of lemonade and sang for him, a little song she'd learned at school, something about good fairies and field mice getting bopped on the head. He smiled. He removed the old glass and set the new panes, quick with the caulk and glazing, humming a bit under his breath. He wiped his mess and put his tools away. Kyla was still in the kitchen, and he caught bursts of paint fumes. He stopped the ceiling fan and duct-taped a penny to the top of a blade to make it balance. He turned it back on, pleased when it spun steady.

Kyla stood at his elbow.

"Mr. Cannon." She had a fleck of paint on her cheek.

"Bob, please." He looked down at her, and his heart gave an awkward jump.

"Bob. Would you like to stay for dinner?"

"We're having pizza!" Gigi yelled.

"Yes, it's fancy-pants dining around here these days. But we'd love to have you."

"I'd like that." He said it quickly, before she could take the offer back.

"Do you need to check with your wife?"

He scratched his ear and shook his head. "She's away."

They sat with their plates on their knees in the living room, the cardboard pizza box on the coffee table. He drank a cola straight from the can. He told her he and his wife were retired now. He told her he had two grandchildren. He asked about her. He sat with his hands on his knees and listened to her talk. As Gigi turned her attention to a coloring book, Kyla told him about her ex-husband, how he came home one day with the news that he was in love with someone else. "It was like I stepped into a ditch, you know. Just, whoops! Down I went, my legs out from under me." She gave a short laugh. She had a freckle under her right eye. A few nods and mmm-hmms seemed to assure her, and she kept talking. She worked at Kyla's elementary school. Just a secretary, she said. It wouldn't be for forever. He liked that phrase, for forever. She was going to take a class or two down at the community college. The ceiling fan pushed a breeze on them, and that's how it felt to Cannon, listening: breezy. Fresh air on skin.

Gigi fell asleep on the yellow pillow, and he looked at his watch, surprised at how late it was. He stood, though he didn't want to.

"What do I owe you?" Kyla smiled up at him. "For the windows."

"Pizza," he said. "And a soda."

"No. Please." She rose and grabbed her purse. "I pay what I owe."

He waved his hand. "It was nothing. It was my pleasure. I enjoyed the work. And the company."

"Next time, then." She shook his hand, leaned forward, and hugged him. Her curls brushed his mouth, and he stepped back, catching his balance.

When he let himself into the condo, Jenny was already in bed. He undressed as quietly as he could, careful not to let his belt buckle hit the tile. He crept under the sheet and curled up against her. Here, in exhausted sleep, she relented. He slid his arm about her waist, calmed by the warmth of her skin. But she was gone at first light.

*

March turned to April. April grew hotter, the smell of the orange blossoms fading. The grass in yards grew thicker. Spindly branches sprouted outrageous purple and yellow blooms. The desert pollen attacked his sinuses, and he carried packs of allergy medicine in his pockets like gum. He changed locks. Jenny tried to swim. The condo smelled of chlorine and mildewed towels. He changed locks. He changed locks.

Kyla did not call again. When he drove by, a Realtor's sign was in the yard.

*

On a late April night, Cannon slid out from bed around midnight, unable to sleep even against Jenny's pliant back. He drove to his properties. The Osborn house was occupied now, a green plastic Adirondack chair on the front stoop. He drove past Montecito and Glenrosa and Indianola. He drove to Heatherbrae. He pulled to the curb and sat a moment with the engine off. The For Sale sign now had an Under Contract slat on top. The flowerbed along the walk held fresh flowers and shrubs. Water glinted on the petals and soil. The windows were dark. Kyla's sedan was parked in the carport. He took off his boots and set them on the seat next to him. He pulled out his keys. In his socks, he walked across the grass to the front door.

He let himself in, quickly, quietly, the lock smooth and precise. The blinds were cracked open, and in the light from the street, he could see boxes stacked along the far wall. The couch and TV were gone. He stepped into the hallway. His eyes adjusted to the dimness. The bedroom doors were open. He walked to the far end of the hall and stood in the doorway. Kyla's room. In the glow of the alarm clock, he could see her shape among the pillows and bedding. A leg kicked out from under the covers. He could hear her breathing. Deep and even. He stood a moment and listened.

He stepped backward down the hall to the other bedroom. Gigi's nightlight was bright, with glitter inside of it, throwing patterns on the wall. The child slept on her back, her arms flung wide, her mouth slack. They could sleep through anything, couldn't they? Robert Jr. was like that. Would fall asleep at football games, in traffic jams, at Cannon and Jenny's poker parties, right in his chair. Cannon would scoop him up and carry him to his bed, tuck him in the cool sheets. He never woke up, a tiny body at rest, calm with primal trust. The sleep of the dead. Cannon held his hands out in front of himself, spread his fingers in the dim light.

The little girl stirred. She sat up in bed.

"Daddy?"

Cannon blinked and stepped forward into the room. "It's me," he said. "I'm here."

She rubbed her eyes. "When are you coming home?"

"I'm home now. I'm not leaving." He stepped closer, a few feet from the bed. "You won't leave either, will you? Do you promise?"

She nodded slow, half-asleep. "I promise," she said, and something in the pitch of her voice startled him, shook him out of his daze. He realized then exactly what he was doing. He stood still, frozen in terror.

"It's just a dream," he said finally. He took a step backward. "Just a dream, honey. Go back to sleep."

"Daddy, don't go." She held up a hand and started to cry.

He moved backward fast. He hurried to the door, quiet in his socks, as Gigi's cries grew louder. He stepped into the night and locked them back in. He started the truck by the light of the moon.

*

When he pulled up to the condo, his headlights flashed on a shiny purple cap in the pool. Three a.m., and Jenny was in the water. He took off his socks and stuffed them in his boots. He stepped out of the truck in his bare feet.

At the creak of the gate she looked up. She folded her arms on the tiles, rested her cheek on her forearm.

He rolled up the cuffs of his jeans and sat on the side next to her. He dipped his feet in. In the pool light, they were as white as caulk, cut with blue veins. His toenails looked thick and yellow. Old man feet. The water felt warm in the cool night air.

She pulled her goggles off and looked at him. "Where were you?"

"Driving. Couldn't sleep."

"Where'd you go?"

"Nowhere."

She lowered her mouth in the water and blew bubbles.

He picked up her goggles and stretched the rubber band. "We have to go home," he said.

"Home," she said. She put her mouth in the water again.

"They're ours, too."

"It's not that easy."

"I know it. Nonetheless. They should know us. Some part of him."

"Which part?"

He shook his head and swished his pale feet.

"Do you want to hear something terrible?" She continued without waiting for him to answer. "I scored it." She hiked up the strap of her suit. The fabric bagged, the elasticity eaten thin by chemicals. "I was standing there at the sink, doing the dishes, picturing it, you know, and I started putting music with it. Like it was a scene from a movie. Piano. Strains of violin."

"Jenny."

She grabbed his calf, digging with her fingernails. "It was an accident. Wasn't it?"

"I don't know." He reached down to take her hand, but she pulled back.

"I can't do this. I can't." She yanked her cap off. Her silver hair stuck up on end, and her eyes gleamed.

He hesitated, but he reached out and smoothed a tuft of her hair. He tugged off his T-shirt, lifted his hips, and slid down into the water. He waded out. His jeans grew heavy, dragging against his skin. He stopped at sternum level, in the middle of the pool.

"Okay," he said. "To me."

"I can't."

"You can. I'm right here."

She stared at him. She turned her back to the wall, braced

the flats of her feet against it, and grabbed the gutter with one hand. "Don't you dare move."

"I won't." He held his arms out to her. "Come on."

He held his breath with her as she threw her arms forward and pushed off the wall. She put her head down and kicked like mad, the water churning. She propelled her arms in a panicked, ugly stroke, her body thrashing like a predator wrestling down its prey. She lifted her face out of the water, shaking it from side to side, her eyes locked tight. She couldn't see that she reached him. He stretched forward, grabbing her hands.

Jenny's chest heaved as she gulped the air. "Don't let go," she got out, panting. She clung hard to his wrists.

"I won't."

He pulled her close. He wanted this to be a good moment, a strand of hope, a tiny victory to counter those endless sleepless nights, those thumbprint, gun-smoke images that lurked behind their eyes. But her body was stiff with terror. She tried to climb his limbs. She pressed on his shoulders and thrust herself upward, trying to save herself by pushing him under. He lost his balance and plunged back into deeper water. He scissor-kicked, his legs weighted with denim, and hot panic shot through him. In the wavery liquid light, they gasped, fumbled, and clawed at each other. Jenny, for God's sake! he yelled. Abruptly, she stopped struggling and went limp in his arms. He kicked hard toward the shallow end until his feet touched the bottom again. He caught his breath as the water lapped at their skin. She pulled back and looked at him.

"Don't," she said. Her voice gave, and her face crumpled.

He started to shiver. He shifted his grasp, cradling her under her back and knees. He waded toward the steps. Floating, passive now, she was nearly weightless in his arms. Like carrying a sleeping child. Like walking on the moon. Lit from below, their bodies did seem unearthly, lunar in their tremulous pallor. He, his wife, and his boy had watched that first moon landing together.

In the darkened, hushed living room, the boy sat between them, his short legs sticking out straight on the sofa. They all watched, wide-eyed, taking in those crackling images, the scratched echo of voices, the bounding steps those men took into the unknown dust. Cannon watched his son's face, illumined by the screen. The boy looked up at him and whispered, Dad, they made it, and Cannon said, They sure did. The astronaut said, Beautiful, beautiful. Magnificent desolation. Cannon then leaped up and opened the curtains, searching for the moon in the sky, suddenly frantic to see that reassuring orb from a distance, to connect the unimaginable sight before him with reality. And when he couldn't spot it, for a moment he remembered thinking, Well, of course it's gone away. They changed it. It won't ever be the same again.

Wrestling Night

Friday night, Clara Teague sits ringside at the Coliseum. Her newly dyed hair floats at the edges of her vision, the red of comic books, of bar drinks, of poofy clown wigs. The chemical stink wafts from her blistered scalp and stings her nostrils, and she catches other smells, too: popcorn, sweat, a dash of hay and dung from past state fairs. In the ring, amateur wrestlers strut in shiny robes and tights, trading grunts and insults. The crowd shouts and chants as The Atom gives a killer knee-drop to his nemesis, Chop Suey Matsui. They bang on the bleachers and yodel and beat their chests when The Flying Swede cuts loose with his signature clogs of death. Clara stays still, quiet as church in her elastic-waist polyester slacks and sensible shoes. The only movement is from her thumbs, which lift and jerk in small circles, a habit of a lifetime.

An hour ago, she had locked herself in the bathroom while her husband of twenty-six years packed up. She had stared in the mirror until she didn't recognize the jowly, underbitten woman reflected there—as her high school students would say, she had

zero clue about this woman. She had found the box of hair dye—
Scarlet O'Haira—under the sink as she searched for a rag and
bleach to clean up her vomit, and she couldn't remember where
or when or why she had bought such a color. As her husband of
twenty-six years shut the front door with a solid click, she bent
over the sink and worked in the paste, the fumes scorching her
eyes. Finally, with her newly seething hair, she wandered out of
her newly empty house in the central Phoenix neighborhood
behind the Coliseum, the corner-lot ranch that she'd inherited
from her parents at age eighteen. In the yard, she yanked spring
flowers out of her prized bed and piled them like animal pelts
until the bed was bare, save for the hulking slab of her husband's
computer screen. The palm trees sagged against the darkening
desert sky, and the orange blossoms sprayed their scent like a cat
in heat. Her dirty thumbs began to twitch. She started walking
and ended up here, at this Coliseum, simply because she heard
the sounds and she followed.

*

The crowd bellows as one Walt "The Butcher" Winklemann
enters the ring wearing a kinky black wig, glittering eye mask,
and blood-spattered apron over a sleeveless black spandex suit.
The Butcher is small and lean-muscled, more cheetah than lion,
but his quick, lethal forearms have made him a wrestling-night
favorite. Even the assholes who torment him at school now chant
mindlessly from the stands, oblivious to his identity, and this
secret revenge revs him up. He stifles a laugh as his opponent,
Slim Jim Jericho, long and lean in leather chaps and cowboy
hat, enters the ring.

Walt can't believe he's here at all. Most of the other wrestlers
on the Phoenix amateur circuit are working men with bristle-
broom beards, married with kids and mortgages; Walt's a senior
in high school, seventeen, and he bags their wives' groceries at
his after-school job and then goes home alone to his geometry

book. When he isn't The Butcher, he is Pansy Ass, Gaywad, Faggety Fag Faggot. At school, he runs or hides when he sees packs of muscled boys in the hall. At home, he is simply alone. Mom works nights as a cashier at Bashas', and Dad is a butcher there. Dad works days, but he heads out to the Indian casinos at night, stopping home only to change out of his stained apron and raid the cash stash. Walt has no friends except for Mrs. T., his history teacher, who lives two blocks down. She lets him stay over for hours after school—he does his homework while she digs in her flowerbed—but she shoos him out when her husband gets home, sending him off with a *Keep up the good fight, kiddo.* He walks the two blocks home, his pockets full of rocks from her flowerbed or napkins from the snacks she feeds him, which he adds to the stash in his room.

One night, flicking through the TV channels, Walt had stopped on the cable access channel: *Phoenix Presents Wrestling Mania!* He opened his front door, and he could see the blue lights of the Coliseum glowing over the palms and hear the cheers in tandem with the TV. He turned up the volume and stared at the masks and glitter and gleaming muscles, at the flamboyant leaps and spasms. He tied on a sheet for a cape, and with walloping chops and seesaw legs, he mimicked those moves. He crashed into furniture and walls, a glassy-eyed boy oblivious to time, space, cold and heat, loneliness. Walt could see the fear in his imaginary foes' eyes as he whipped toward them. Towering over them, his pigeon chest puffed, he made them pay for their insults, their pummeling, their indifference.

For weeks, he watched the matches and practiced on the dock behind the Encanto Park boathouse or in his crammed bedroom, honing his freakish speed and strength. He perfected his knife-hand chop, the flapjack, the clothesline, the flying somersault and baseball slide, the leg sweep and neck snap. In his small, silent world, he grew stronger, skilled and lightning-fast, until one day he tried out for wrestling night. No one saw him coming.

*

Clara Teague pushes back her shoulders and clears her throat, watching The Butcher romp around the ring in his mask and fright wig. He looks like a kid, not much older than her students with their relentless needs and barbecue chip breath. She realizes she hasn't thought of her students all day, though normally they can take up whole days and even nights, but now she can't even summon them. After all, her divorce won't even be a blip on their radar. Her life is nothing to them.

She looks at The Butcher's swift young arms. His skin is as smooth as a ripe, unsplit watermelon. Just starting out, all the potential in the world. She'd met Stony around that age, long before he'd become *Stony Teague*, poet and professor of prominence. Stony had been in her first college poetry class. At nineteen, with her parents dead within a year of one another—Papa of heart failure, Mama crushed inside her Galaxie by a speeding delivery truck on the interstate—Clara watched her college peers from the outskirts, alienated by her warped entry into adulthood. She owned a house. She paid insurance. She ate dinner alone every night on a mahogany table that seated eight.

After class one night, Stony surprised her on the stairs outside. With his thick, kinky black hair and even thicker black-rimmed glasses, his lumpy hips, he reminded her of a roly-poly bug—one flick and he'd curl up around himself. He reminded her, well, of herself. He squinted at her with his hazel, myopic eyes and held up one pudgy hand. In that small gesture, Clara's thumbs began their twitch. She ran to those stairs, to their future relationship, clomping in her enthusiasm and thick shoes. She latched on to Stony Teague with the fervor of missionaries, a blind, almost autistic love.

*

In the ring, Walt tries to calm his thudding heart and short breaths. He reels dramatically from Slim Jim Jericho's high-flying roundhouse, rolls silver-quick from Jim's hang-gliding slam off the ropes. Slim Jim's one tall, skinny bastard, and he gets some air, his fringed chaps and vest aflutter. The crowd chants *Butcher, Butcher*, and Walt raises his arms in a menacing V. He flies at Slim Jim, pummeling with ferocious speed. He grabs Slim Jim around the neck and shoulders and holds him tight to his chest, breathing in the smell of burned tobacco.

An hour earlier, when Walt had arrived at the Coliseum, Jim was leaning against the wall by the entrance, still in his street clothes: a T-shirt, faded jeans with a hole in one knee, and scuffed brown boots. Walt's stomach had fluttered. He has confided in no one about his longings, not even in Mrs. T. Certainly not in his parents or schoolmates—as if he would give his asshole tormentors more ammo.

Jim held out the cigarette pack to Walt, a wordless hello. Walt didn't smoke, but he took one from the pack anyway and let Jim light it.

"Ready for tonight?" Jim said.

Walt said, "Think so." He leaned next to Jim, puffing and trying not to cough.

"Don't be too hard on me in there," Jim said. He punched Walt on the arm and cracked a grin. Smoke escaped from his mouth in a curl. "You go to Central?"

At Walt's nod, Jim said, "Yep. Me too. Back in the day. Wasn't my scene." Jim looked at the tip of his cigarette as if analyzing it for clues. "You and me should hang out sometime."

Walt stopped himself from saying, *Me?* He tried to sound casual as he answered, "Sure."

Then Slim Jim caught Walt's eye and held it for four heartbeats, until Walt felt heat in his stomach. With a smile, Jim broke the gaze and crushed his cigarette beneath his boot. "See you in the ring, kid," he said.

Walt nodded and smashed out his own cigarette. He lifted his fingers and held them to his nose.

In the ring, Walt reels from Jim's sharp elbow in the ribs, and he turns and runs. Flight. His first instinct. Jim starts to chase him around the ring, and Walt remembers the first day he met Mrs. T.: fleeing down her street, flinching as fistfuls of pea gravel hit his back, the pack gaining on him. Then Mrs. T. popped up out of her flowerbed, all fuzzy brown hair and flashing sunglasses. Walt veered up her driveway, his short legs chugging.

Mrs. T. yelled, "Stop, you little rat bastards." She held her rake overhead and tromped down the driveway, calling his tormentors each by name and threatening to call their parents. They scattered down the street and into bushes.

Mrs. T. squatted down and squinted at Walt, and she gave a brisk nod. "You're all right."

He nodded, hiccupping and wiping at the sudden tears.

She leaned close enough that he could smell her peppermint breath. "You're one of the good ones, I can tell," she said. "Do you want a soda? Come on. Come over here and help me with this planting. I've got a whole flat of petunias. Gardening takes your mind off things." She held out her rake to him.

He stared at the rake in her dirty palms and then up at her face. The sun set her wild brown hair afire, a warrior princess. She seemed taller than he could ever imagine. He took the rake, felt the wood scrape the pads of his fingers. Later he would sneak it home and prop it in the corner of his room with the rest of his possessions. For now he lifted the stick over his head like a scepter, and he vowed to love her forever.

*

The Butcher's arms wrap around the neck of Slim Jim Jericho, whose cowboy hat has fallen off and whose face is turning purple. Clara thinks of Stony, of doing that same move to him until his head pops clean off. She savors the image of his thick glasses shattering on the cement, his salt-and-pepper head rolling down the front steps of their old home, smashing into pulp at the bottom. She imagines scooping up the mess with a flat shovel and using it as fertilizer. She imagines cooing pigeons feasting on brainy flesh. Bile rises in her throat.

She found out that afternoon in the stupidest of ways—she stumbled on their emails. She saw her friend's name and opened it, naturally, because the woman was *her* friend, or at least longtime acquaintance—a plump, pretty coworker, seven years younger, with whom she shared rides and school gossip and news about Stony's achievements. It was this woman, in fact, who had driven Clara to the doctor when her final miscarriage hit during fourth hour at school. Clara had blinked at the computer screen in a long, blank moment of incomprehension: Why in God's name was her friend sending a poem? A pornographic poem?

Stony confessed to all of it, the length and breadth of the years-long affair. He couldn't wait to drop that heaving cardboard box of lies he'd been lugging around. As he talked, Clara kept trying to think back, to pinpoint what she was doing when it first happened. She would have been adding to her flower garden, transferring her coddling tendencies to the earth. She'd have been driving the same used Honda, teaching at Central High, where she'd always taught. She'd have been cleaning house and mowing the yard and buying groceries and driving to meetings and giving lectures on the Taft-Hartley Act and grading tests and patting students' shoulders and helping Stony with mailings, typing his manuscripts, making copies, keeping his increasingly busy schedule. She'd been happy to do it, to be part of something.

On and on a repentant Stony rambled, and as she watched his fillings glint with saliva, she realized that somewhere along the line he'd grown accustomed to having the stage. Talk, talk, talk. People clung to his words, boosted his ego into preposterous volumes. He was no longer that stubby college boy but instead a distinguished presence. He held court.

He blinked at her from behind his still-thick glasses. He said, "There was no one else."

"Just one, then." She laughed, the crack of breaking bones.

"Tell me what to do, Poodle," he said. "Tell me what you want me to do."

She stared at him, at the reality before her. She'd spent twenty-six years of her one and only life on a lie. Her existence was reduced to something out of a bad poem. She was that woman. Poodle. She stared down at the computer monitor, still blinking with its sordid news. In one spurt of adrenaline, she pulled it from its desk moorings, lugged it down the hall, and heaved it, like a bag of drainage rock, out the front door. Then she gagged and ran to the bathroom.

The boisterous crowd chants for The Butcher, who's thwapping Slim Jim about the neck and head, and Clara shivers with a sudden sense of déjà vu (when was she last here? at the state fair? when?), but the moment slips past before she can grasp it. Something grows large and aching inside her, travels up her spine, slides into her scalp, throbbing with the chemicals. Her thumbs resume their flutter, matching her hummingbird heart.

*

Slim Jim ducks and picks up Walt by the legs, heaving him over his long back, and Walt braces himself for a wicked pile driver. His head meets the mat, and he lets out a lung-bursting howl, vamping up the convulsions. He rolls fast to his feet and lets out a long growl. Here, with his mask and gaudy costume, he is something beyond himself, bigger, strong, unbelievably quick. The matches are staged, but sometimes he lands blows and sees the surprise in his foes' eyes: *Well, what have we here.* Even the painful jolts he himself takes, the black and citrus-yellow bruises and occasional vomiting, are worth it. The best moments come in the finale, his victory laps and bows, the brief moment before he goes back to being the pasty kid who watches TV alone, who bags groceries with Mom, who hides out in the gym equipment room. He wishes he could capture those finales somehow like butterflies, put them in glass jars with holes poked in the lids so they could breathe. He'd hoard them in his closet at home, in his graffiti-tagged locker at school. He'd put one next to his father's laundry basket. He'd give one to Mom to keep at her register. He'd give a shoebox full to Mrs. T. to line up on her school desk, on her mantel, so that people could see. They'd see.

But the moments don't last. They fritter like ash, gone as soon as the spotlight careens off to the next contenders, and Walt walks home alone, his costume stuffed inside an old pillowcase. So Walt drags out the action in the ring, hams up the pratfalls, feigns injuries and comebacks. Tonight, with Slim Jim, it is a strange, violent dance, shuffling feet and jousting hands, chests pressed close. Walt presses closer, breathing hard. He gets as close as he can.

*

Clara shifts on the arena bench, smooths the tops of her slacks, barely registering a jolt from the elbow of a cheering woman behind her. She pictures Stony at the little dive bar at the end of McDowell, where he'd confessed he often met up for pints with Clara's friend and his graduate students. She can see him there among the bar regulars, the old jukebox flickering and pulsing. She can see her friend there, too, her sausage fingers resting on his forearm. Clara blinks hard until the image disintegrates, and she refocuses on the ring. Her thumbs flutter as she watches those boys circling, landing their bone-crushing blows. The ring pulsates with exaggeration and silliness, like a carnival show, and moments come flooding back, rushing over her until she can taste salty sweat on her lip.

Her house is behind the fairgrounds—she remembers when this sway-backed Coliseum was built, flooding the neighborhood with a lovely blue light. When the state fair came every year, she would sit in her backyard and watch the light filter through the mesquite tree while inside Mama and Daddy played cards with the neighbors. She'd catch smells of the cotton candy and the Indian frybread with powdered sugar sold on the thoroughfare, bursts of music and squeals. Her mouth was full of braces trying to fix her underbite, and her worn Capri pants bagged around her knees. Her head was full of the overzealous poetry that she scribbled, of far-off city skylines. She would smooth her frizzy hair and watch the top of the Ferris wheel flit through the tree and think of the large and waiting world, of far-flung places full of sea salt and whitewashed hotels and scattered languages. Her heart pulsed and her unpolished thumbs twitched at the thought of when her day would come.

*

Walt is scheduled to be tonight's winner, and the ringmaster gives him a sign. With a final slingshot catapult into the ropes, Walt jumps up and clotheslines Slim Jim, knocking him flat. Slim Jim falls down for the count, giving Walt a quick wink. Walt puts his foot on Slim Jim's chest and raises his arms high over his head. He smiles until his cheeks ache, looking down into Slim Jim's lightning-bright face. They lock eyes again, and in this exquisitely blind moment, Walt can't see that Jim is simply curious, that they will have a mere two months together until Jim marries a cross-eyed girl named Beatrice whose groceries Walt will then bag—they will eat a lot of canned stew. He can't see that he will take up smoking, puffing and inhaling, gasping at the acrid smoke, keeping close the smell of first love. Or that wrestling night will be over in six months, a fad driven into the ground by bad management, and that he will work at Bashas' as a cashier like his mom for the rest of his life, a steady and decent income. Or that over the years, he will sleep with dangerous men dangerously, getting his heart broken again and again and again because he is too needy, too clingy, he wants too much, because he cannot help himself, trapping them, hoarding them, because he wants—needs—to believe. Or that he will die of lung cancer—not AIDS, as many of his asshole classmates assume—at the age of forty-four.

He can see none of that. Right now, standing in a sweat-stained wrestling ring, Walt "The Butcher" Winklemann quivers with happiness. He feels it in him like a transfusion—new blood, humming loud with life.

*

Clara stares at The Butcher, standing so puffed and posed. Holding court. She feels a crack in her sternum. Her thumbs stop whirling, and the frenetic twitch moves to her legs. She gets to her feet with the rest of the crowd. She darts over the security bar and pulls herself into the ring, rolling under the ropes. Then she is on her feet and running straight at The Butcher. She tackles him against the ropes, a red-haired dervish in polyester slacks. With closed fists, she starts whaling on his puny chest.

Walt puts up his hands, guarding his face from the sudden attack. The woman's hair is an unholy red, bright as blood on snow. He realizes with a slow, dumb blink that it is Mrs. T. He tries to push her shoulders, to grab her wrists. "Mrs. T.," he says, "Mrs. Teague, it's me, Walt. It's me." But she doesn't hear him or the bewildered silence of the crowd. She keeps coming, all knuckles and sharp nails.

Walt rips off his mask and wig. "Mrs. T., it's me."

She stops as fast as she started, dropping her fists. Walt. Her student, Walt Winklemann. She stares at him in a long, confused moment. She asks, "What are you doing here?"

"It's okay," he says.

She blinks, and the truth of her life comes rushing back. She winces at the lights, the crowd.

"Walt. Oh, God." She feels her knees give, and she starts to fall, staring with wide eyes at the boy. She can't see beyond his face, this day, this moment. She is engulfed in her pulsing halo of pain. In this moment, she can't possibly imagine that with her divorce settlement, she will retire early and travel for months on end, her hair as bright as the sangria that she will drink by the tumblerful. That she will sell her old house for a ridiculous profit and move out of this old neighborhood and send Walt Christmas cards and postcards with stamps from far-away countries—*Keep fighting the good fight, kiddo.* That she will embark upon a few short-lived yet shockingly sexy and gratifying romances overseas. That she will travel and scribble in journals and substitute-teach for the sheer joy of it until she is old and wrinkled and wispy on the scalp, resorting then to gaudy, angular wigs. She can't imagine that she will outlive Walt and see his obituary in the paper one morning over her coffee and weep, her eyes full of this long-ago wrestling night and of the boy's sweet face and for what he did next in that ring, the thing that might be the beginning of what saves her.

Up close, Walt sees how pale Mrs. T. is. He sees the blisters on her scalp, the puffiness of her eyes, her dirty fingernails. All he can think to ask is, "What's wrong?" but she is going down, and he doesn't have time to think, much less speak. Fast as ever, Walt grabs Mrs. T.'s elbow, pulling her up. The crowd murmurs now, gaping. Someone recognizes him and calls out *Fag* in a knee-jerk hee-haw. Slim Jim has rolled away to the corner, agog like all the rest. Walt holds Mrs. T. up by the elbow. She is deadweight, shaking, and she seems so small, too small. She opens and closes her mouth but says nothing, dazed and hooked on his arm. She should be taller, he thinks. She is taller than this.

Impulsively, Walt grabs Mrs. T. around the waist and hoists her up to his shoulder. With a slight stagger, catching his balance, he leans into the ringmaster's microphone and says, "Ladies and gentlemen, introducing The Scarlet Tornado!" Holding her around her knees, Walt begins to walk the perimeter of the ring. She's as light as a butterfly. Light, so much light.

The crowd erupts, and Clara looks down on the boisterous throng. From her perch, the people are a deafening, swaying, open-mouthed sea. They're *cheering*. For her. For Walt. She looks down at Walt's small, wide-eyed face, and she lets out a surprised hiccup of a laugh. He grins up at her, red faced but steady on his strong legs. She pats his head, squeezes his shoulder, and he holds her up. For a brief moment that night, under the heavy lights and applause, they shine like naked beating hearts. They pulse and shine, pulse and shine, exposed to the eyes of the world.

Meet Me Here

Two years after Zoey's father died, her mother got a face-lift and a tummy tuck. Zoey didn't find out until they met at the airport for their trip to Austria. "Surprise!" her mother said. She posed, strutted for a moment, and ran her hands along her flat, almost indented stomach. Inexplicably, she said, "I almost didn't have the doctor put in another navel." This image was so bizarre and terrifying that Zoey's right eye started to twitch. She looked at her mother's shiny skin, at the sliver-moon welts that ran from her temple to her jaw, and she felt a hitch in her knees. Her husband, Ben, grabbed her elbow and pulled her up. He said, "Wow, Clare, you look great," and kissed his mother-in-law's new cheek.

For seven days in Austria, Zoey followed her mother from shop to shop, sight to sight, and then slept hard in the narrow hotel room with outlets that didn't fit their hairdryers. On their last day, they took an early train to Salzburg. At the Salzburg train station, her mother stopped at an information booth and rummaged through maps and brochures while Zoey sat on a bench, frizzy haired and sleepy, stretching out her sore calves.

From her coat pocket, Zoey pulled out one of Ben's telegrams, which had been coming daily. Such a weird, endearing thing to do in the email age. It read, *Minor fire in toaster oven. No sign of cats. Recaulked bath. Going to have a yard sale.* She bit her thumb. Ben was an archaeologist, but he did home projects when he was upset. They'd been married three years, together for five, and in that time he'd learned to tile and plumb and rewire. When Zoey was upset, she obsessed over details. The week before this trip, she'd finished her freelance graphic-design assignments and then rearranged the living-room furniture into right angles, organized the closets by colors, alphabetized and labeled the refrigerator shelves, and started memorizing fonts. She ran her finger over the type of the telegram. Palatino.

At the airport, Ben had kissed Zoey on the mouth and whispered in her ear. "Call. We'll have international phone sex. You can fake it from all the way across the Atlantic."

She'd dropped her hands from his shoulders. "That could be the last thing you say to me."

He ran his hand through his hair. They had been up all night, arguing about having babies (he wanted them, Zoey didn't anymore), which devolved into bickering about who *always* left the back door unlocked (Zoey) and who *always* made the coffee in the morning (Zoey!). The circles under his eyes were like thumbprints.

She picked up her duffel and set it down. "At least give me something worthy of an airport."

Ben put his hands in his pockets. "You've been watching too many movies."

She shrugged, looking at a stain on the gray industrial carpet. She picked up her bag again and walked toward the checkpoint. Ben grabbed her sleeve.

"Take pictures," he'd said. "Ones with you in them."

Zoey's mother sat down next to her on the bench, armed with

brochures and maps. Her metallic-blue wraparound sunglasses were propped on her head, and her new lime-green headphones hung around her neck—a *steal* on eBay. Since she'd retired from her job as an office manager, Zoey's mother had become an Internet shopping junkie. Things arrived in Zoey and Ben's mailbox daily—movies, CDs, a palm-sized camera, collectible Pez dispensers.

Her mother pointed at a brochure with a picture of a medieval castle and told Zoey, "That's where we're going first. Then the house where *The Sound of Music* was filmed. That movie came out right after Dad and I were here for our honeymoon. The whole movie wasn't filmed at the house. They used the front of it and the lake outside. You know the scene where the kids fall out of the boat?"

Zoey ran her fingers along the brochure and on Ben's telegram. It was her first time in Europe, and her husband was all the way in Phoenix, Arizona, setting the house on fire, losing the cats, and hawking their clothes and chipped dishes. She was with her widowed, surgically enhanced, Internet-savvy mother, clomping around foreign streets with her dead father's teaching pension.

"Franklin Gothic," she said.

Her mother looked at her, and Zoey guessed that she frowned, but she had no lines on her forehead. Zoey touched her own brow, her Pensive Brow, Ben called it.

Zoey pressed at her face, feeling her puffy eyes under her sensible black sunglasses. Her face was tight and dry, and she rubbed the back of her hand against her chapped mouth, a moisture trick that her science-teacher father had taught her years ago. He'd explained it with a pop lesson on the layers of the skin—epidermis, dermis, hypodermis—and then he pinched the tops of their hands to demonstrate the effects of age: Her skin snapped back like elastic, his stayed puckered.

Zoey pushed her sunglasses up her nose. "What *day* is it?" she said.

Her mother stared past her. "There's still so much to see."

Zoey looked at her mother's profile and then turned away quickly. In a certain light, her mother looked like someone else—a beautiful, tight-cheeked stranger in a foreign country. Earlier on the train, the weak sun had cut white swaths on her mother's oil-smooth cheeks, taut even in sleep. Zoey had reached out and traced the new scars near her mother's jaw and ears, an old one under her chin from when she'd crashed a scooter as a kid. She had put her hand lightly on her mother's chest and watched it rise and fall, something she'd done often when she stayed with her after the funeral, fearful that her mother would go too—heart disease like him, or a brain tumor, an errant lint ball lodged in her esophagus. She'd leaned in and lifted her mother's headphones, but she could hear nothing. She fought down the aluminum taste of panic, looking at her mother's hands, at the large knuckles and wedding band embedded in the skin. They, at least, had not changed.

*

Zoey and her mother climbed the steep route to the Hohensalzburg Castle, holding their coats tight against the wind. At the top, they wandered through dim rooms and courtyards. Her mother stopped at the gift shop, and Zoey waited outside, sitting on a wall that overlooked the city. She took Ben's first two telegrams from her coat pocket and read them again. *Back from dig. Cats have gone missing, must know something I don't.* The second one said, *What are you wearing?* She smiled and rubbed the type. She used to go with him on shorter digs when she was between designs. He dug with his hands in the flat, dry earth, the fan of his back like a cobra, dangerously sexy. He unearthed *her*, and she couldn't get enough of him. Lately, though, she stayed home. She worked alone in her office with the cats sleeping on the daybed next to her, or she rented movie after movie until she was tired and foggy from crying. When he came home, she was happy to see him. She loved him. There was no question of that.

She heard her mother laugh loudly, and she looked up. Her mother was talking to a man and woman who were both wearing Arizona State sweatshirts. She called, "Look, Zoey, look!" Her voice was booming, and Zoey felt that panic again, as if she'd realized she didn't have her purse. Her mother looked like someone Zoey might vaguely recognize on the street. Hours later, she'd snap her fingers: That's it! She's my mother!

The couple her mother was talking to were about her mother's age (the age she should have looked, fifty-eight), empty nesters, kids off to college. They both were a little overweight, a lot gray, and loaded down with bags and camera gear. The lettering on their sweatshirts was Britannic Bold. They waved and turned away, their heads together, the woman holding on to the man's sleeve.

Zoey's slim, frosted-blonde mother in hip-hugger jeans and black leather coat walked up and leaned on the wall. She started pointing out the rivers, Mozart's birthplace, the Mirabell Gardens. She hopped up on the wall and opened her arms wide.

"Isn't this amazing?" her mother said. "What a view." She took her tiny camera from her pocket and snapped a picture.

"Mom, sit down before you fall."

She did a fake wobble and turned the camera on Zoey, who ducked her head inside her coat.

"Dammit. I'd like one picture of you. Just one."

"I have a problem with cameras. How many times do I have to tell you this?"

Her mother sighed. "You and your father. You know how we have so few pictures of him? That should be a lesson to you." She handed the camera to Zoey, who took the picture as her mother smiled and threw her arms out wide. Zoey could see the old scar under her chin.

Her mother sat back down on the wall. "I took that same picture of Dad. Caught him by surprise."

Zoey remembered the picture among the others in their albums: her father looking over his shoulder, his mouth open, a lock of hair sticking up in the wind. In her father, Zoey could see herself: tense shoulders, Pensive Brow, same gray-green, wide-set eyes. That was one of the things Zoey hated about photos: They didn't do people justice. People became replicas, strange versions of themselves. In her own wedding pictures, she looked tense and squinty, as if someone had elbowed her in the nose.

Zoey fiddled with the camera. "You seem happier now."

"Yes, well. Grief is a strange thing," her mother said. She rubbed the back of her hand against her mouth.

Zoey kicked the wall and looked up at a bare, sprawling tree that shadowed the ancient stones. "That's not what I meant. I meant, you're happier *now*. Without him."

"I know what you meant," her mother said. She pressed her firm cheeks. She looked at her hands and put them in her pockets.

*

They had lunch at a café overlooking Mozart Plaza. Zoey smoothed her hands over a wine list.

"Myriad," she said.

"What?" her mother said, unfolding her napkin.

"The font. Myriad. Very clean."

The waiter set down their plates, refilled their coffees, and dropped the check in one smileless motion. He had started to walk away when Zoey's mother said, "You know, you look a little like Gregory Peck. In his dashing days."

The waiter blushed and let out a high-pitched giggle. Zoey blinked in amazement. Her mother sipped her coffee, smiling.

Her mother leaned over to the couple next to them and asked to use their salt. She started talking to the woman, who was pregnant. She told her, "Take lots of baths. You couldn't get me out of the water with this one. Couldn't keep clothes on me either." She put her hand on Zoey's and squeezed it, hard, her rings digging into Zoey's knuckles. "Someday I'll talk her into giving me a grandchild." Zoey looked at her sandwich and coughed. The pregnant woman smiled and nodded, bewildered, and turned away.

"Now she's picturing you naked," Zoey said.

"What's wrong with a little conversation?"

"They're strangers. You know, they're having lunch. They don't need to know my ovarian cycles."

"Or maybe they like what I have to say."

"Probably. That must be it."

Her mother let out a disgusted sigh. "Sometimes, I swear. You're just—" She looked into her cup. Zoey's eye twitched.

"I'm what?"

"Speaking of ovarian cycles."

"We weren't," Zoey said. "We weren't speaking of them."

"What, a mother can't ask about grandbabies?"

"No, a mother cannot."

"I'm not getting any younger."

"Oh, I wouldn't say that."

"Funny." She fiddled with her wedding band.

Zoey reached over and pinched the top of her mother's hand, watching the skin stay raised. Then she pinched her own—it didn't snap back so much as settle down for a nap. Epidermis, dermis, hypodermis. She rubbed at the patch of skin and said, "Not anytime soon."

"Does Ben know this?"

Zoey sighed. "We can't seem to talk about anything else these days. It seems everyone wants me knocked up. Oh, for the days when the goal was *not* to get knocked up."

"You're not getting any younger," her mother said.

"I'm only thirty."

"Those eggs have a shelf life, you know."

"Maybe we could put them up on eBay."

Her mother rolled her wrinkle-free eyes. "The point is, it gets harder the longer you wait."

"Do you remember that flour-sack incident in high school?" Zoey had dropped her family relations "baby" when she was opening her locker. Its soft, white guts spilled all over the orange industrial carpet. "I'm not ready. I'm not sure if I ever will be ready."

Her mother waved her hand. "No one's ever ready. They just do it and get it over with."

Zoey stared at her. Her mother pulled a lipstick from her purse, applied it, and looked out the window. A pigeon landed outside and pecked at crumbs. She said, "Are you ready? The *Sound of Music* tour starts soon."

"I think I'm going to skip it," Zoey said.

Her mother looked up. "Why? It's not that far from here."

"I'm exhausted." It was true. Zoey was so tired she couldn't see how she was going to get out of the chair.

"Oh, come now. You're young. Hup hup."

Zoey frowned and narrowed her eyes. "First I'm not getting any younger, and now I'm young. Which is it?"

"Don't get smart."

"Look, I'm just not all that interested, okay?"

"Well, that's the problem with your generation." Her mother blotted her lips with her napkin and looked at the pink smudge. "What do they call you, Generation X? You're all profoundly uninterested. Incapable of caring for anything beyond yourselves."

"That is a gross generalization. I don't *have* a problem. And I care about a lot of things." Zoey's neck grew hot, and she heard her voice rising. "For instance, I care about the fact that I seem to be living in a twilight world where my mother doesn't seem to notice, or *care*, that her husband of thirty-seven years is dead or that she's turning into some kind of plastic surgery freak. But no, no, I do not care about the Von Fucking Trapps or a musical where people are singing all over the goddamn place."

People turned in their chairs, glanced over their shoulders. Zoey's mother stared at her, blinking fast. "I see," she said. She balled up her napkin and started throwing things back in her purse. She stood up, bumping the table. Their water glasses shook. She said, "You know what? You're *blind*, Zoey. You're so goddamn blind. You can't see beyond this." She waved a hand in front of Zoey's face. "Maybe it's a good idea if you don't have kids."

The waiter hovered next to them, his eyebrows knitted in concern. "We're fine," Zoey told him. She put a hand over her twitching eye. "Let's go."

"No," her mother said. "You stay here. You stay here and do whatever it is that you do." She put on her coat and checked her watch. "Your freak of a mother is going to see her stupid house. Meet me here at four. The train leaves at five."

Zoey held the handles of the chair, the metal back hard against her spine. Her sandwich sat high in her belly like a ball of red yarn. Her mother buttoned her coat and started to walk away but turned back. Her flawless face contorted, her eyes bright with tears. She pointed at Zoey and said, "And it's a love story. It makes people happy. And what is wrong with that is what I'd like to know."

*

Zoey wandered through Salzburg alone, standing on bridges, looking in shop windows, running her fingers along buildings. Her boots echoed in the stone walkways. Without a map, she kept an eye on the river to track where she was. In a souvenir shop, she bought three bags of memorabilia, maxing out her credit card. She found a pay phone and called Ben. She woke him up.

"Did the cats come back?" she asked.

"MIA," he said. "It's 5:00 a.m. here, Zo."

She breathed onto the metal phone and ran her finger through the condensation. "I bought you a beer stein."

"Spill," he said, yawning.

"I had a fight with Mom. Sent her into a tailspin." She leaned her head on the phone and watched a woman across the street drop an armful of folders. Papers scattered, rising on the sharp wind. Zoey pressed the back of her hand against her mouth and rubbed. "I don't understand why she can't be more—" She stopped, her throat tight.

Ben said, "Lost? Falling apart?"

"No. Yes." She slumped against the phone window.

"Hey," he said. "Hey, love."

"It's been two years. Everyone else is fine. She's fine. She's totally fine."

"No, she's not. She's doing it the only way she knows how." He sighed. "He wasn't her dad."

She wiped her nose on her sleeve. "Maybe I'm not equipped."

"For what?"

"Existence. Parenting. All of it."

He exhaled into the receiver. "You're equipped fine. You have all the equipment."

"Uterus, check. Vagina, check. Wide birthing hips, check."

"For Christ's sake."

She took off her shoes and stood on the sidewalk in her socks. "Say I have one of those days. 'C'mon, sweet pea, get in the car. Tuesday is Mommy's therapy day!' Or say I leave the front door open. I mean, the cats right now are loose and terrorizing flowerbeds across Phoenix. Tiny little people don't just get out. They suffocate, they drown, they bruise, break. Or they grow up and end up sitting in the middle of a café in the middle of Austria saying horrible things to their mother."

"Zo."

She whacked one of her shoes against a pole, and mud chunks fell to the cement. "Say I get hit by a bus. Say my heart gives out. And there's this tiny little person, she's grown more now, maybe with my eyes and your terrific nose, and I'm gone. Or you're gone. Gone, gone for good."

He coughed, and the bed squeaked. "Look, I don't have the answers. I don't. I can't promise you that none of that will happen.

The whole goddamn thing is a crapshoot. Live or die, live or die. You live, you love, you hope for the best."

Her feet started to go numb. "That's oversimplifying it, don't you think?"

Ben wheezed a little. "It is simple," he said. "Sometimes it really is that simple."

*

After Zoey hung up, she took off walking and got lost. She went up and down a zigzag of streets and alleys, trying to find the river, fighting down the panic. Who was that vaguely familiar woman on the street? That's it! It's me! In her head, she recited the only German words she knew: Danke, Bitte, Glockenspiel, Hefeweizen. Near the castle, she took another turn and ended up in an old cemetery. She sat on a bench under a sweeping pine, breathing hard, trying to figure out which way to go.

The cemetery was quiet except for a few tourists and a family tending one of the plots. The two children played some kind of game, walking the brick around the grave like it was a beam, while a woman dug a fresh place for flowers. The graves were lush and neat, decorated with Baroque crosses and headstones. The inscriptions were ornate and in a font she didn't recognize, one full of serifs. She tried to decipher names, dates, and epitaphs on the headstones but gave up and closed her eyes. The inscriptions probably read much like her father's. Beloved Husband and Father. In Our Hearts Always.

She pulled her knees up. She started to do the skin test that her father taught her, pinching and pushing at her hands, her crow's-feet, the backs of her arms, the scarred ridge on her shin from when she crashed her bike and Ben got on his knees and wiped off the pebbles and blood with his T-shirt. She pressed her navel, her teeth, muscle and sinew and bone, checking for resistance. She read the foreign words around her and for some reason thought of the night she got caught sneaking out to meet a boy when she was fourteen. It was the night her mother told her about sex for the first time.

It hurts, her mother said. It hurts, and then it gets better.

*

Eventually, Zoey found her way back. She bought a map and got halting directions from a man at a gift shop who was surly until she told him he looked a little like Gregory Peck in his dashing days. Then he sent her on her way with a free cup of coffee. But she was late getting to the plaza. The café was closed, and she walked among the pigeons and meandering tourists, straining to find her mother's blonde head. She finally saw her standing in front of the Mozart statue. She recognized her immediately this time. Even from that distance, even with the changes, when it came down to it, Zoey could pick her out of a crowd without hesitation. She could, she realized, find her blind.

Zoey stood in the middle of the plaza under the weight of her things, and she watched her mother. Her mother was posing, letting a stranger take her photograph. Zoey recognized the statue then—it was in one of the pictures from her parents' honeymoon. That picture was of both her mother and father, years before she was born, when they were skinny and gawky, new at being grown-ups, new to love. Her father had a full head of hair, an arm around her mother's waist, squinting and shy, a pen in his pocket. Her mother wore white cat-eye sunglasses and a beehive hairdo and had her head on his shoulder. Now, for this picture, her mother stood with her hands on her hips, wraparound sunglasses pushed on top of her head. Her chin was at an angle, tough and jaunty and splendid. But she also looked so small, leaning there in the half-shadow of a legend.

Zoey started to run, her bags banging against her legs. She called out, "Wait, wait for me!" Her mother shielded her eyes and held up a hand. Zoey dropped her bags, out of breath. They looked at each other for a moment, and then Zoey stepped into the picture.

She put her arm around her mother. "You're shrinking."

"Funny," her mother said. She leaned closer.

The man raised his hand. "On three," he said.

Her mother lifted her chin, her smile as wide as the day. Zoey held on to her mother, digging her fingers into the cold leather of her coat. The camera flashed, and it was done. A moment of their lives captured in one simple click. As her mother thanked the man and gathered her belongings, Zoey was thinking about how someone else—say, a child, say, *her* child—might talk about this picture years from now. She could see it quite clearly: a teenage, gray-green-eyed version of her and Ben, sitting on the couch with a boy, a photo album across their laps. Zoey's daughter taps the plastic-coated page and tells the boy: That's my mother. Can you believe it? Look at how *young* she is. And what is with that hair? Hellloooo, Earth to Mom, it's called a hairbrush. Zoey's daughter runs her finger over the photo, across her mother's face. She says, She told me once that when it was taken, she was thinking about me, about having me. That's all she said about it, and that of course she was happy, that she just takes bad pictures. Which is true. God, it doesn't even *look* like her. Pictures never do her justice, you know? She always says she wishes there was a way to do people's lives a little more justice.

Water at Midnight

Sunny waited in the dark yard, the water cool on her feet and ankles. She wore an undershirt and boxer shorts that she'd stolen from her father's dresser. The thin cotton shirt hung loose on her small shoulders, and she'd folded the elastic waistband of the baggy shorts down twice. She bent at the waist, splashing the water on her legs, all that water that smelled like the creeks and ponds she swam in back home, a fleeting swamp in the desert June night. She wet her arms and neck and waited for the man who irrigated their yard to come back. She was seventeen.

The man came into the yard through the back gate. Sunny had been watching him through her bedroom curtains since May, when her mother sent her to her father's house in the heart of Phoenix, because she was often up late reading or couldn't sleep. Sometimes she would see him look at her window. His name was William. She had seen it on the irrigation bills that she found in the mailbox when she checked for letters.

William leaned down and closed the big irrigation valve, his black rubber boots shiny in the water. He stood up and stretched, rolling his neck. He saw Sunny then, ankle deep in the middle of the dark yard, the last one on his route. She lifted her arm and said, "Would you like some tea?" She said, "I'm Sunny. I made some iced tea."

She brought two glasses of peach iced tea to the back porch, a book of matches tucked into the elastic of her shorts. Her father had not stirred when she cracked his bedroom door and looked in on him. Her father slept like the dead. He was in bed early and up ages before Sunny got up, so the only time they saw each other was at dinner and on weekends, which was fine with her. The times she did see him, it was one question after another, and she was tired of making up lies about where she had spent her days, about being *productive*.

Sunny handed William a glass and lit the lantern on the wrought-iron table. She sat in the porch swing across from him and pushed with both feet. "I can't believe it's still so hot out."

"Summers are long," William said. "This is my last stop." He took a long drink of tea and set the glass on the concrete. He looked at her bare feet. "You're up kinda late, Sunny."

"Oh, I'm good. Nights are good for me." She put her glass between her thighs and swung.

William looked around the yard at the giant ash tree and oleanders, at the bicycle propped against the wall. He knew yards by foliage and furniture, the ones that were mowed or not. He knew the styles of homes. At one point in his life, before he took over his father's irrigation business, he wanted to study architecture. He wanted to restore old homes. This one was a 1940s ranch, the brick unpainted and in good condition. The porch wasn't original, maybe added in the sixties. Someday he would like to buy a home like this. He pointed to the child's swing set against the left fence. "Did you grow up here?"

"No, that was here. I just moved here." She dragged her feet on the cement. "The woman who lived here before died, you know." She smiled at him. "Do you think her ghost is still around?"

William leaned forward and shrugged. "Sure. Ghosts are every-where." He drained his tea, the ice cubes falling against his mouth. Condensation dripped onto his jeans. "I should be going." He stood and pulled his shirt down. "Thank you for the tea."

Sunny pushed the swing and held her legs out straight. "Anytime."

She watched him slosh back through the water, water that would be gone in the morning, soaked into the grateful earth. William turned and waved as he went out the gate. Sunny lifted her hand and held it up until she couldn't hear his footsteps in the alley.

William set his boots on the floorboard of his truck and drove home in his bare feet. The bottoms of his jeans were damp, and he rested his arm on the open window. The air grew warmer as he drove out of the irrigated old neighborhoods in this city he grew up in. The sky was barren, and he wished the monsoon would come and break up the days and nights with rain and dust, even a good power outage.

When he went into the apartment, his wife called out his name from the bedroom, startled, and he said, "It's me. I'm home." He dropped his boots on the tile. In the kitchen, he opened a beer and drank half of it without taking a breath. In the bathroom, he splashed water on his face and ran his hands through his hair. In the bedroom, he sat on the edge of the bed with his hand on his maybe-pregnant wife's back and watched the ceiling fan spin. He would not sleep that night. He would watch the sun rise through the blinds. He would make juice and toast for his wife before she went to work at six. He was thirty-two.

*

Sunny was waiting for William again two weeks later. The light was on in her window at midnight when he opened the valve in her yard, and he stood there, feeling the water rush over his boots, watching the window for movement. It was 3:00 a.m.

when he returned to shut the valve down. Sunny had set up two chairs in the middle of the yard under the ash tree, the metal legs submerged, and she held two glasses. William checked his watch and rubbed at the stubble on his jaw. He sat next to her, the chair sinking down, and Sunny handed him a glass of tea.

He drank, his elbows on his knees, his eyes on the dark windows of the house. The porch light shimmered across the water, glanced off the shadows around them. Sunny sat cross-legged, her father's T-shirt pulled over her knees. She watched William tug on his baseball cap and wipe his brow. He reminded her of the new character on her soap opera, which she had started watching daily. She used to watch it only when she was home sick from school, but now she had nothing better to do. She uncrossed her legs and dipped her feet in the water.

"It's so hot." She moved a foot next to his boot. "I can't get used to it."

He leaned back and pulled at the brim of his cap. "You will."

She bit her lip and kicked the water, looking at her toes. She had painted them a bright cherry red. She said, "Where does all this water come from? I mean, I know the canals, but before that."

William pushed his feet forward and felt the soft ground under his boots. "The Colorado River."

"Huh. I've never been to Colorado."

"It runs through the Grand Canyon," he said.

"I know. I've never been there either."

"You should."

She lifted her shoulders and frowned. "It's a thing with me, I don't know. I lived an hour from it, but it always seemed so overrated. I guess I haven't done a lot of things."

"You've got time." He had been to the Grand Canyon twice, once alone and once with his wife and her family, but it had been a long time. It had been a long time since they had a vacation at all. He chewed on an ice cube and watched Sunny move her feet in the water.

He said, "Shouldn't you be out with your friends, drinking at a desert party or something? I grew up here, and that's what we did."

"I don't have any friends." She tucked a piece of hair behind her ear.

"You should."

"Well, I will." She poured out her tea, and the ice cubes floated around his feet. She stood, holding the empty glass in both hands. "You don't have to patronize me, you know. You could talk to me like a normal human being."

She walked through the water toward the house. William watched her go. Her hair swung against her back, and her T-shirt gave off a faint white glow. He set his half-full glass on her empty chair.

He unlatched the gate and turned to look at her window. The curtains were open and the light was on. Sunny stood there, hair down around her bare shoulders, T-shirt in her hand. He stepped back and gripped the cool metal latch. She held the T-shirt against her chest and pressed her hand against the window. He thought he saw her smile before she moved back and the lights went out.

*

It was August before William saw Sunny again. All of July, he watered the ten neighborhoods that he and his partner handled, stopping his truck on the dark streets and going into sleeping strangers' backyards. He knew these streets well, the neat brick homes and the wide grass lots. They were like the ones where he and his childhood friends lived, where they rode bikes and built forts in the oleanders before the city boomed and spread at the edges.

When he was a boy, he helped his father do the irrigation in the afternoons after school. He followed his father around with a rake and weed cutters and cleared out overgrown grass and valves choked with burrs. Most of the year, they irrigated during the days, but in the summers, his father would go out long after dinner, and William wouldn't see him until late the next day. When he was old enough, his chore became their own yard. He would go outside in his boxer shorts while the rest of the city slept, the air thick with the scent of orange blossoms, and reach down and let the water rush up to meet his hands and feet. He would doze on the old couch on the back patio, and he would drink cold milk and jack off, thinking about parties and girls and where he might move after high school, somewhere far, far from all those hot, watery days. He thought about those big homes on the East Coast he'd seen in books, with their wrap-around porches and lighthouses in the distance. He saw himself on a sailboat, headed out to sea. When the yard was flooded, he would crawl into bed and fall back into the free, thick-breathed sleep of youth, staying there until the sun was high in the sky.

Summers now were the hardest. His wife called it Survival Mode. They kept the blinds closed in their apartment. She complained about wearing pantyhose. She started counting the time down on a dry-erase board on the fridge: *99 days until I can see you. Love, Me.*

William watched her get dressed in the early mornings before he fell asleep. One morning, he helped her zip up her dress and rested his hands on her back. We should take a vacation, he said. This October. I think it would be good for us. She turned and kissed his cheek, rubbed at the stubble. You know we don't have the money. Especially now. She stood and ran her hands down her dress, pressing at her belly.

July was long and it was hot. It was the time of year when people carried umbrellas to keep the sun off, and cars sputtered and died on the side of the freeway. The monsoon clouds stacked and taunted them from the east but never brought rain. At Sunny's house, William leaned against the back fence when he was finished, his skin and clothes damp, the water still under his tired feet. He chewed his fingernails and cuticles, leaving them raw and red, something he hadn't done since he was a teenager. He watched her window and looked for movement in the curtains. When the porch light flipped on, he stood up a little straighter and put his hands in his pockets. Then he went home to his not-pregnant wife and curled up against her back. Sometimes he made love to his wife there in the early mornings, the fans on high, the sheets stuck to their skin, and she said things like, This time will be it, I can feel it, and all he could smell was canals and heat.

For her part, Sunny stayed in the house. During the days, she slept late, and her father left her lists of chores and money on the fridge. She vacuumed and then took a nap or watched her soap opera, the air conditioner cranked down too low. She got mad at the main character for lying to her boyfriend, the best guy she'd ever had. She held the remote control and pressed out numbers on the buttons—her birthday, her old phone number, the date of the day at the clinic, the month before her mother shipped her off to live in a strange city—until she hit one that sent the TV into a tailspin, snowy and hissing in the silence of the room. She waited for the mail, watching the mailman come up the sidewalk, and her heart beat a little faster. But he brought only bills and sweepstakes offers for her father, which she filled out and sent off, along with the letters she had written in her uneven print on her father's yellow legal pads. Her mother called and talked into the machine while Sunny sat on the couch in her underwear and masturbated or picked at her dry feet, dropping the strips of skin behind the sofa. Her mother didn't tell her father about that day at the clinic. She told Sunny, It would kill him. Lord knows I can't stand the son of a bitch, but *this*. Her mother said things into the answering machine like, Are you being good, Sunny? Give me a call. I miss you.

Sometimes, after searching through her dad's files and taking quarters from his dresser, Sunny rode her bike to the library or to the Circle K for Diet Coke. One day, the liter of soda fell off her bike rack and exploded, fizzing and hissing on the hot pavement. She got off her bike and kicked the bottle, watching it streak and foam across the asphalt. She chased it and kicked it again. Fuck everyone, she yelled at a passing car. She sat down on the curb, the cement burning the backs of her thighs.

On irrigation nights, Sunny watched in the dark from the kitchen window. She sat on the counter with her feet in the stainless-steel sink and turned the faucet on and off in time with her father's snores. She watched William lean on the back fence. She reached to turn on the porch light, and when she turned on the garbage disposal by accident, she flinched and lifted her feet. She hunched her shoulders and listened, her breathing a little faster. Her father kept snoring. She flipped on the porch light and saw William push himself off the fence and disappear into the alley.

*

On that August night, the moon was half full, moving in and out from behind dense clouds. To the east, lightning flashed behind a great swell of gray. William found Sunny waiting on the swing set. The house was dark except for the porch light, and she swung slowly, holding the chains, her bare knees turned in. Her face looked puffy, as if she had been crying. "Hey," she said.

William sat in the swing next to her. It was too small for him. The chains and seat pinched his legs.

"Are you all right?" he asked.

Sunny nodded, her hair falling into her face. "My dad and I got into a fight. It's nothing."

"What about?" He looked at her face, at the tiny mole on the underside of her jaw.

"Oh, I don't know." She pointed at the house, and her wrist cracked. "I should get a job, I should think about what I want to do with my life."

"I wouldn't think you'd have to know now."

"Yeah. Well, I have no idea. New York, maybe. That's what I told him and he flipped." She lifted her feet, leaning back in the swing. "He's an engineer."

"New York, huh. Well, that's something. I'd like to go there myself."

"It seems like there's something bigger out there, you know? There should be something bigger than this." She waved her arms at the yard. "I'm not sticking around here, that's for sure."

William nodded. "I know what you mean."

They swung in silence, the water rippling around their ankles.

"Any sign of the ghost?" William asked.

Sunny smiled. "Nope. And I've been looking, too." She kicked at the irrigation water. "I wish we had a pool. I guess I could swim in this."

"I doubt it's safe." He took off his boots and set them on top of the slide. The water soaked the bottom of his jeans. "I could use a swim myself."

Sunny twisted the swing, moving her knees side to side. "My mom has a pool at her apartment. I used to sneak in at night. Or we'd go to the creek."

"Why aren't you there now?"

She shrugged and stood up, rubbing her arms. She looked at her father's dark window. "I got in trouble," she said.

Sunny moved in front of William and sat down in the water. She lay back and tried to float. The water covered her, ran in her ears, and she could feel the grass under her legs and shoulders. Her T-shirt swelled with air. She pressed the bubble flat, kicked her legs, and sat up, her hair dripping.

William looked at the T-shirt stuck to her skin, at her small breasts, her nipples dark and hard. He said, "Better?"

"Not much." She pushed her hair off her forehead and leaned back on her hands. She crossed her ankles and looked up at the sky. "There are never stars here. Back home, they're everywhere."

William looked at her kneecaps poking out of the water and then at the dark sky.

She gathered her hair over her shoulder and twisted it like a rope. "I have to start school here soon," she said.

William thought of his wife's board on the fridge. He was down to day 28. "I remember starting in August. I didn't have a car, and there was no air conditioning on my bus."

"Great. One more thing to look forward to."

"It's not so bad. Think of all the friends you'll meet." He nudged her foot.

Sunny pressed her knees together and scooted forward until her feet were between his. "Yeah, right. All those girls with new lipstick." She scooped water and watched it run through her fingers. She put her shins against his. "All those boys who either ignore you or try to jam their tongues down your throat."

William gripped the chains of the swing. He held his feet still. "It gets better," he said, and Sunny shook her head. "It does." He lifted his hand toward her and dropped it. He rubbed at his jeans.

Sunny put her hands around his calves and pulled herself up. She stood over him, water dripping off her shirt onto his legs.

"And I'm telling you it doesn't." She pressed her hands on her stomach. "I can feel it."

He pulled his feet underneath him and pushed his toes into the dark, wet earth. Thunder rolled somewhere in the shadows of the sky, the flashes of light moving closer. He flexed his palms on his knees, the chains tight against his elbows. "I hope that's not true."

Sunny leaned forward and bumped her knees against his. The tips of his fingers brushed her skin. "It is," she said. She pulled her shirt up over her hips and wrung out the cotton. He could see her ribs, the slight muscles over her navel. He looked at his boots sitting on top of the slide.

Sunny watched his throat move, and she tied her shirt in a knot around her waist. She hooked her thumbs in the top of her underwear and rocked on her heels. William looked at the grass sticking out of the water around the base of the slide and then at Sunny. He leaned forward and rested his thumbs on the insides of her knees. Thunder cracked loud and sharp above them and Sunny jumped, her thighs flexing against his hands. She stood still and curled her hands on the sides of her legs. She started to shiver, her shoulders jerking. William moved his thumbs, felt the fine hair above her knees.

She looked down at him and bit her lip. "Do you think." She cleared her throat and closed her eyes. "Do you think anyone could ever love someone like me?"

William looked at Sunny's shadowed face, at her small shoulders curved forward like a quarter moon. He thought of his wife at home, sleeping the way she always did, with one leg kicked out from the covers. He thought of his wife's steady breathing, the way she pulled at her lip when she was worried, the way her skin glowed in the blue-gray dawn. He dropped his hands. "Yes. I do."

Sunny opened her eyes, and she smiled. She started to say something when lightning flashed bright and swift above them. She looked at the sky and then at her father's window. The light was on. Rain started to fall, landing in uneven, fat blotches on their arms.

Sunny stepped back, looking at the window, and she untied her shirt. "I have to go," she said and turned, almost running through the water. She disappeared into the back door, and the porch light went off. William put on his boots in the night, holding the slide for balance.

*

It was October when William saw Sunny again. Until the end of September, when they started watering during the day, he'd switched routes with his partner, taking the neighborhoods farther south and east, learning new trees and swing sets, doghouses and patio furniture. His still-not-pregnant wife had started to make him shower before he came to bed, deciding that her flat belly and periods had to do with the canals. You smell, she would say and turn her head into the pillow, pulling her knees up into her chest. On the board in the kitchen, she wrote her grocery list and underlined the doctor's appointment for the next week in orange dry-erase marker.

On that October day, he drove his truck down Sunny's street and stopped two houses down from hers, a file folder of bills and a stack of travel books from the library on the seat next to him. She stood with her bike in her driveway, her backpack slung on one shoulder. She was talking to a boy. The boy had spiky blonde hair and had his hands in his pockets. He dragged his sneaker in a half-circle on the cement. Sunny laughed, her head back and mouth open. Her teeth were white against her tan. She didn't see him there two houses down in his truck, hands gripped tight on the steering wheel. She didn't see him start the truck and do a U-turn in the middle of her street and drive away, both windows down to catch the October wind. She didn't see him hook his arm over the door, adjust the side mirror until she was only a speck, tiny and fluttering. She didn't look at all.

Any Sign of Light

On their first date, Sam Stone and Ruby Jamison sat on the hood of his truck next to a boarded-up transmission shop in south Phoenix. They were on their way to the state fair downtown, but a fire near the interstate jammed up traffic, so they took side streets and stopped to wait it out. The fire was in a factory of some kind, only a half-mile or so from where they parked, in the part of the city where farmland and citrus groves wearily resisted development, the wide streets patchy with houses and strip malls. From there, the downtown skyline looked fake, a stage set built in a vast, empty theater. They sat on the hood of Sam's old truck—his first vehicle ever, with its busted right taillight and passenger window that left a gap wide enough for a child's hand—and they watched the fire grow in the twilight. The air smelled like burning plastic or hair, and it made their eyes itch. The smoke billowed in earnest, the dense, blackened orbs climbing on top of each other like drowning victims.

Few cars passed them in that dim parking lot, and they sipped on bottles of beer that Ruby bought at the convenience store across the street. Sam was twenty and Ruby was thirty-one. They worked together at a small restaurant near the university in Tempe where he was a cook and she waited tables. Sam was starting his second year at school, and Ruby was taking two classes. All she could afford, she told people, but she thought she might like to be a teacher someday.

Ruby asked him that day if he wanted to go to the state fair after shift, and he said yes, quickly, because there was something about Ruby Jamison that made him speak too quickly. It was something about the way her bangs were too long and got stuck in her eyelashes, the way she chewed her pens, even the way she licked her fingers after she refilled the ketchup bottles. All day, the thought of being alone with her made him need to sit down. Just the idea of getting out of his apartment was enough to make him hurry through his prep work. He didn't get out much. Usually, he stayed home and watched TV, clicking through reruns, movies of the week, talk shows, news channels.

Sam shivered a little in the cool October air. The news helicopters buzzed over the fire, and sirens flashed, a chaos that echoed. In the distance, traffic stood still on the freeway, a glinting mass of exhaust and taillights. He fiddled with a bottle cap on his knee and looked at Ruby out of the corner of his eye.

The other waitresses, girls who used their tips for beer money and shopping, didn't like Ruby. They slouched against the walk-in in the kitchen, their slanty mouths full of clam chowder, and talked about her, about her unfashionable clothes and her tangled hair. Can you imagine? they said and rolled their incandescent eyes. Just shoot me if I'm waiting tables when I'm that old, they said. Sam didn't say anything. He didn't like those girls. He had slept with some of them, but he didn't like them. Sam had gotten laid a lot in the last few years, after he got his pacemaker.

Those girls liked Sam because he was quiet. He let them talk, and he didn't talk much at all, which they thought meant he *listened*. He laughed at all the right times, and he said wry things—he was so *funny*—and he waited. Then when they were, say, sitting at the bar after closing and telling him their secrets, and they finally said, *What about you?* that was the moment. He rubbed at the spot below his left collarbone where the pacemaker showed through his thin T-shirt. He lowered his head and told them, *I have a bad heart.* He took a deep breath and stuffed his hands in his pockets. Their mouths softened. They looked at his skinny shoulders, his small face, and at the square plate that pushed his skin up, and they said, *Aww.* Eventually, they led him to their beds and fucked him, benevolently, on top of flowered sheets. In their candlelit, poster-filled rooms, he pretended that they were being filmed for a love scene. He cupped their faces, their necks, their arched backs, and he whispered in their ears. In his mind's eye, he could see that he was there, flesh on flesh, but it never felt real to him, even as he felt the heat grow in his limbs, even as they touched that place on his heart like a talisman.

With Ruby, it hadn't gone that way at all. She didn't talk much, for one thing, and when she did it wasn't about herself. She talked about music, she was crazy for music. She handed off tapes at work, saying, You've got to listen to this. Sam took them home to his small studio apartment, where he played them over and over on a stereo he picked up at the thrift store for fifty bucks.

"It's really going, isn't it," Ruby said.

Sam looked at the flames. "It is," he said.

He drank his beer in long swallows, feeling light-headed. The Velvet Underground played on the truck's stereo, and Sam pretended he knew the songs. He nodded along, patting his knee.

"I hope no one's trapped inside," Ruby said. She pulled a cigarette from her shirt pocket and lit it. "I quit, you know."

"I can see that." Her fingers were as long and slim as tree roots. She wasn't soap opera pretty, or even talk show pretty. She was more hand-soap commercial.

Ruby pulled an inhaler from her pocket, took a hit, and flipped her cigarette over the front of the truck.

"I should put that out. Wouldn't want to start a fire," she said. She laughed at this and slid off the hood, grinding the butt under her sandal.

Sam watched her hips shift, and he sat up straight. He rubbed his eyes and looked back at the fire. Helicopters hovered, shining strips of light across the smoke. The flames jumped erratically under the black, and the dense mass seemed as if it was moving closer, coming at them. He looked up at the sky. He imagined planes circling behind the smoke, heavy and hovering, wasting fuel, but he couldn't see any sign of light.

Ruby waved her hands in the air and frowned. "What in God's name are we doing out here in this? It's probably toxic."

Sam shrugged and rubbed his neck. He wondered what building the fire was in, what was burning inside of it. He thought of that one movie, where an arsonist set traps for firefighters behind doors, how the fire *breathed*. He thought, Someone could be dying. His heart thumped, and he reached up and tapped the plate on his chest automatically, that foreign object inside of him.

"Living dangerously," he said. It sounded ridiculous, and he hoped she didn't hear him.

But Ruby smiled. She didn't smile much. Her teeth were crooked, the left eyetooth jutting. Sam wanted to rest his finger on it.

She said, "Well, let's hope we make it out alive, then."

She shook out another cigarette, smelled it, and tucked it behind her ear. She leaned on the hood and hitched up her skirt, watching the sky.

"Hey, look at that. The Ferris wheel." She pointed toward the skyscrapers downtown, and Sam saw it spinning through the haze. He shivered again. He didn't ride the Ferris wheel. He was afraid of heights. He got vertigo and couldn't even walk next to railings above the third floor.

Ruby said, "I used to go to the state fair every year as a kid.

I'd take quarters and dimes from my mom's old water jug and spend the whole day there."

Sam stared at the spinning colors and thought of the time he messed around with a girl behind a dime-toss tent at a carnival back home in Massachusetts. He was sixteen and had had the pacemaker all of three months then. Before the surgery, that smart, silky girl wouldn't have noticed him, let alone talked to him. Before the surgery, he would have been at home with his parents watching sitcoms and eating TV dinners. He remembered the girl's cotton-white breath in the late fall night, the damp, deep heat of her as they moved their hands inside each other's jeans, until a man called out "Hey you kids!" and they flew apart, buttoning their clothes as they ran.

He said, "You grew up here?"

"Most of my life. We lived up north with my grandmother for a little while, but mostly here. Then I left, and now I'm back."

"Where'd you go?"

"That," Ruby said, "is a long story."

She kicked at the ground and looked at the front of the truck. "Oh, Sam, bad news." She pointed at the grille. "We hit a bird."

Sam bent down and peered at it. It was wedged low, between the fender, a mass of beak and head and feathers. He recalled the moment he must have hit it—he had thought it was a paper bag swirling across the road.

Ruby said, "I saw this nature show on PBS last night. It was all these moths and bats and spiders, and how the prey developed defenses to ward off the predator, and the predator developed ways to counteract them. Like, the moths made up this false sonar, so the bats grew larger ears. The narrator said something about predators and prey can't evolve without each other."

Sam raised an eyebrow. "Okay."

"It just reminded me. Dead animal, PBS."

Sam squinted at the bird. It could have been a clump of leaves or a mud clod, not a dead thing. Hitchcock's movie *The Birds* popped into his head, people running for cover. He reached his hand toward the grille but pulled back, his stomach fluttering.

Ruby said, "I think you're going to need a power washer to get that out." She patted his shoulder. "The tape stopped. I'll flip it."

The dome light kicked on, and Sam watched Ruby through the windshield. She held up a tape, her tongue between her teeth. He touched his own tongue to his front teeth, feeling the partial cap where he'd cracked one on a soda bottle when he was a boy.

Sam walked around to the driver's-side door and leaned his elbows on the open window. "'Pale Blue Eyes,'" Ruby said, turning it up. She hummed along, mouthing some words. She sat in the middle of the wide seat, her head back.

"That's a nice song," Ruby said. "My mom, God knows she has her faults, but she used to always have music on. Not so much like this, but Joni Mitchell and Fleetwood Mac. You do know Joni Mitchell, yes?"

"Sure," he said, although he didn't. His parents never had much music on. His father watched television, so Sam knew a lot of theme songs. He could still recite jingles from his childhood.

"Hey," she said. She pulled herself forward on the dash. "What color are your eyes?"

Sam's eyes were brown, like dirt, or maybe cooked hamburger meat. He blinked, thinking of his face in the mirror in the mornings. Sometimes he would stand there and look at himself, trying to see how others see him, until his face became a stranger's, someone he might vaguely recognize in the grocery store. In the sky, the smoke was as thick as pavement, impenetrable. He wished his eyes were that color.

"They're just brown, I guess," he said.

"Come in here a sec. Let me see."

Sam climbed in and put his hands on the steering wheel. Ruby turned down the music.

"Open." She leaned in close. Sam could see the fuzz on her cheek and that the cigarette behind her ear was broken at the filter. She wheezed a little. She smelled of smoke and lavender soap.

"They're brown, all right. But nice. Very soulful." She tilted her head. "Like a deer, maybe. What's going on in there, I wonder?"

Sam moved the steering wheel with his knees and touched his plate. Her eyes were cat-hazel, changing from green to yellow to brown like autumn leaves.

Ruby flipped off the light and sat facing him, her feet next to the gearshift. Sam looked straight ahead. The sky was dark, but the smoke had started to make a strange, orange shine. It reminded him of snowstorms back home, that night glow, the world hushed and eternal.

She took another hit off her inhaler. "It feels like someone's sitting on my chest."

"Sorry," he said. He rolled up his side and looked at the gap in her window. "Sorry."

"You don't talk much." She pulled her feet up, tucking her skirt between her thighs, her bare knees jutting.

"No," Sam said.

He rested his forearms on the steering wheel. He lowered his head.

He said, "I have a bad heart."

Ruby held her knees, rubbing her thumb on the left one. She gave him a long look. She said, "That makes two of us."

"No," he said. "I mean for real. I have this." He pulled down the top of his T-shirt and tapped the pacemaker. "See?"

Ruby leaned close and ran her finger along the scar. She pressed at the plate.

"That's wild," she said.

Sam looked at her hand on his chest and felt something warm swell inside of him. Ruby rested her head on the back of the seat. She pulled at a string on her skirt and stared out the window. Then she looked at him.

"Jesus. You're twenty years old."

"So?"

"There is a distinction, you know. But you don't see it because you're twenty."

"It's not like I can help it," he said. "Besides, I don't relate well to my peers."

She smiled, her fang tooth jutting.

He said, "I know a few things. I pay attention."

"All right," she said. "Let me ask you this: What is the one thing on this earth that you would die for?"

A helicopter circled close by, its searchlight sweeping the empty lot to the left. Sam thought about the firefighters in the building. Maybe they had found someone inside the factory, someone who was working late, someone whose family was waiting at home with supper growing cold on the table. He pictured one of the local TV newscasters, some blonde woman looking serious, saying, We know five are missing.

"I don't know," he told Ruby.

"Oh, come on. That's not true. What about family? What about," she said, and put her hand on that spot on his chest, "love."

Sam swallowed and looked at her hand. His heart picked up speed like any old regular heart, one that worked free of science, one that functioned off the soul, but it made him panicked and disoriented, as if he was called on in class. Sweat broke out on his lip. He thought about those girls and how they smelled sweet, how they said his name into his ear, how they turned their backs to him when they hooked their bras. He thought of his parents, asleep by now in their twin beds, the glow and faint hiss of the TV filling their room.

"I'm not sure about that," he said.

"Yeah. It's complicated." She leaned closer and pulled down his collar, rubbing her finger along the plate. "It's never like you dream it will be."

She dropped her hand and dug in her bag for another tape. She held it up.

"This is Lucinda Williams. Listen."

Sam rested his chin on the steering wheel and listened to the guitar and the words and the singer's scratchy voice. Bits of white ash landed on the windshield, and Sam pressed his thumb on the glass.

"What about you?" he asked Ruby.

"What about me, what?"

"What would you die for?"

Ruby shrugged and coughed. Her breathing sounded worse, almost a growl. She pushed in the car lighter. She pulled the cigarette out from behind her ear, snapped it in half, and dropped it on the floorboard.

"I had a baby girl once," she said. "I would have died for her, but she beat me to it." The lighter popped out. She held it close to her palm and touched the skin, brief and searing. She bit her lip, rubbing at the mark.

"I'm sorry," he said. He felt small enough to slide under the steering wheel, even under the brake pedal.

Ruby finished the last of her beer. She turned up the volume on the radio. "Listen to this part. This is a great part."

Sam listened. He pulled the last beer from the pack on the floorboard and twisted it open. He rolled down the window and flipped the cap out, breathing in the acrid air.

"Her name was Rose Marie," Ruby said into the dark. Her voice was low, and she took short breaths. "She was the most beautiful thing you ever saw. I had a husband, too."

Sam handed her the beer. She took it but didn't drink. She picked at the label, flicked a piece of it to the floor. Her shoulders were hunched so far forward that he thought she might fall over.

Ruby held up a hand. "I don't know why I'm telling you this. It was a long time ago. I was your age, come to think of it," she said. "I guess it's not something you grow out of, though."

"That must be hard."

"Some days," she said. "Some good, some bad." She rubbed her thumb over her knee again. "The good news is, the rest of the bullshit pales in comparison, you know? Sex, religion, politics, money, lousy breaks. All those things that you thought mattered or shaped your existence or whatever, they don't."

Sam thought of all the things he was afraid of. Needles. Strangers. Serrated knives. Flying. Heights. Heights especially. He was shamed by those things then, and his face grew warm. He put his hand on the gearshift and moved it back and forth.

"I wish I were that brave," he said.

"I'm not brave," she said. "Some days I can barely open my eyes."

"Still," he said.

Ruby took a sip of her beer and wiped her chin. "What would you do if you were?"

Sam looked at his hands on the steering wheel. They were shaking, and he put them between his knees. He bit his lip and stepped down on the brake pedal. In the rearview, he could see a red flash from the one good taillight.

He lifted his hand, and he ran his fingers down the side of Ruby's neck, feeling the tendons, a mole near her ear. He touched her jaw, the dent in her nose, the hollow at the base of her throat. He touched her tooth. She tilted her head so that his hand was in her hair. He turned and moved closer so that he could use both hands. Under her shirt, her collarbones were sharp, her pulse was fast, and he put his mouth on them, and her breasts, and her navel. She tasted of salt and flesh and heat. He pressed his face into her, listening to her strong heart and the thickness in her lungs. And her hands were there, too, tangled with his. They were on his face and his chest, pulling at his clothes and at her own.

Ruby said something Sam couldn't understand, lifted her skirt, and moved on top of him. She held the back of his neck, and he closed his eyes. He lifted his hips to hers, and she sighed. With his mouth against that perfect pulse, he started to imagine himself a different person. First he gave himself a new body, tall and brown and without scars, a young man who could use a microwave and pass through airports unheeded. In this body, he ran every day around the college track in cutoff sleeves, and people stopped to watch him. He rode glass elevators, pressed himself face-first against the glass and watched the world from that great, shining distance. In this body, he played guitar and wrote songs that Ruby sang in the shower. And he was there, too, with her. He washed her back, and they stood together until the water grew cold, until they were both clean and shiny-new.

He opened his eyes. Ruby moved above him, her eyes closed. He looked at his skinny arms, his pale hands on her breasts, and realized that this was happening. He was having sex in a sweet old truck with Ruby Jamison, the girl with the bad lungs, *the* girl. She was like nothing he had ever seen before, and he laughed, short breathed, incredulous. The music drifted and the sky burned. She said his name—*his* name—and her body started to shake. Sam listened to her jagged breathing. He smelled smoke and felt something like the sun in his throat.

Ruby pressed against him, and he listened to her heart beat, first fast and then slower. She coughed, sat up, and opened her eyes. She ran her thumb across his eyebrow and over the raised plate on his chest.

"There's your heart," she said. She put her face in her hands and shook her head. She coughed again, her shoulders up around her neck.

"Don't say anything," she said.

Sam nodded. He licked his lips, tasting her salt.

She stayed wrapped against him for another minute or so, her breathing slower. She climbed off him and pulled down her skirt. Sam buttoned his jeans and shirt, his hands unsteady.

They sat and watched the sky, adjusting their clothes, smoothing their hair. Sam couldn't see the flames anymore, only smudges of black and streaks of light from the helicopters. A siren whined in the distance. The tape ended, whirring. Ruby wheezed. Sam touched her hand, but she pulled it away. She lifted her bag from the floor and started digging through it.

"I've always hated this part of a tape," she said. "That empty lag."

Sam listened to the blank whirring. For some reason, it reminded him of the end of a movie he had just watched, where the boy goes to get the girl and the camera focuses on the boy's car and the wide-open road while the credits roll.

Ruby sat back. She looked at the roof and then at him.

"Maybe we should head back."

He shook his head. "We could still go."

"I don't think so."

"We could ride the Ferris wheel," he said, his voice rising. "We could buy some cotton candy and hand over a bunch of tickets and ride the thing until they kick us out."

"Look," she said. "Let's not do this."

"No, really. We should go. We should ride it." His voice got higher, and his stomach twisted at the thought of sitting in the metal bucket, of that lurch when it stopped at the top, the world shimmering beneath his feet.

Ruby said, "It's not going to change anything."

Sam swallowed down on the acid rising in his throat. "It might," he said.

Ruby ejected the tape and put another one in. She blew her bangs out of her eyes and ran her finger along the condensation on the windscreen, drawing a face and a stick body. She turned and put her hand on his arm. Her fingers were cold.

"I was giving her a bath," she said. "I set her in and went to check a load of laundry." She looked at him, blinking fast. "Laundry. Can you imagine?"

"No," Sam said. He couldn't.

She said, "Take me back, okay?"

Sam reached forward and turned the ignition. The engine started, but he misclutched and stalled it. He cleared his throat and felt something slip and give, like a bag of groceries falling out of his arms to the pavement.

Sam turned the key again. The engine caught, and the truck rumbled. Sam revved it, and Ruby turned up the volume. She said, "Bob Dylan. 'Blood on the Tracks,'" and Sam remembered the bird.

"Wait." He let the engine idle and got out of the truck. The smoke was heavy, almost human in its weight. The convenience store across the street looked dazed, its neon signs alien. Sam kneeled down on the gravel in front of the truck. He grabbed the bird and pulled, the feathers soft and cool in his hands, and his heart beat a little faster. It was a wren, and its head fell to the side, but its body was whole, no blood or gashes, just a tiny bird that flew too low in the dusk. Sam held it in both hands and walked to the side of the abandoned building, looking for a good place to put it, that thing that looked as if it were sleeping, just trying to find a place for its head. Before he laid it down, before he and Ruby headed back to where they had started, Sam wondered what would happen if he stood up and let it go, if he raised his palms and tossed it to the wind. He lifted it to his face, and the feathers brushed his mouth. He told it, *Fly*.

At the Terminal

Francie should have had a suitcase. Something in understated tweed, perhaps, or maybe one of those old hardsides with a matching train case, or a rolling duffel at least. At her age, she should have worn a better outfit than a T-shirt and baggy denim overalls and better shoes than her canvas sneakers. She fiddled with a strap on her faded red backpack, rolling the nylon in her fingers the way she used to roll cigarettes until she'd quit two months earlier. Her burgundy modified bob, blow-dried straight that morning right before Clive said, *We need to talk*, now frizzed in the damp Seattle air.

She was three hours early for her flight home to Phoenix. Since she didn't have to check luggage, she waited on a cement bench outside the terminal, where city buses hissed and groaned and exhaust fumes mingled with the odor of potted vincas and geraniums. A late-summer storm had blown through, and she shivered in her short sleeves—in Phoenix, it would be over a hundred degrees. The sky was still dark, the clouds discordant, dropping rain in light, skittish bursts. Rainwater dripped from the roof onto the concrete, plop, plop, plop. Francie kept her sunglasses on and shoved a wilted tissue underneath them from time to time. She looked up, and a drop of water landed on her forehead—plop.

Francie took out her cell phone and dialed her sister, Jean. Francie had met Clive, indirectly, through Jean: She had bought Francie a DSL connection and Internet dating subscription for Francie's thirty-fourth birthday.

On the night of Francie's birthday, Jean had handed her the gift certificate and said, "Now, don't freak out."

They were washing birthday-dinner dishes at Jean and her husband's house in Tempe near the university, where Jean was an assistant professor of anthropology and working on a study of single women in the twenty-first century. At thirty-two, Jean was married *and* up for tenure. Francie worked as a hair colorist, a now-four-year career that her mother and father, both economics professors, called a *delayed backpacking trip to Europe*.

Francie said, "I'm not your guinea pig, Jeanie."

"No, you're my sister. And you need to get out of the house."

"I like my house." Francie rented a one-bedroom guest house, where she stayed in on weekends, listening to the same CDs for weeks at a time, where she ate soup with her face too close to the bowl, where she locked the door the second she was inside and checked it again in the middle of the night. The part she did like was the dark, grassy backyard, from which she could see stars and planets. She'd been tracking the progress of Mars since August because she had read that it was closer to Earth than it had been in centuries. She'd sit out there with some Johnny Cash or Steve Earle on the stereo, and she felt safe, happy even, looking up.

Jean said, "I'm telling you now, honey, it doesn't like you. When was the last time you had a date? Don't make me ask about sex."

Francie frowned. It had been a year, for both. Bad first date, bad sex, bad hangover—the trifecta. She bit her lip, trying to remember the guy's name, and cleared her throat. "Okay, so you give me a gift where I won't leave my house. I'll sit in a dark room, chain-smoking, while some guy gets off to my picture."

"It's not like that at all." Jean squeezed soap onto a sponge. "It's anonymous, yes, which is the paradox of social interaction in a technological age. And yet, it harks back to old courtships in many ways. Letter writing. Except faster."

"Like Jane Austen on speed," Francie said. "Like Simone de Beauvoir to Sartre, but not."

Jean, a woman with no patience for irony, flipped soapsuds off her hands. She gave Francie a look that Francie took to mean, *And you wonder why you don't date.*

Francie touched her sister's hair. "You need your roots done. Maybe some highlights."

Jean knocked her hand away. "Just think about it." She picked up a plate of cupcakes and the coffeepot and headed for the dining room. She stopped and looked back. "I'm *worried* about you. You used to be fearless."

At the terminal, Francie listened to the cell phone ring and watched people unload from a blue shuttle van. Two flight attendants with matching chignons stepped out with their tidy luggage carts. Francie touched her frizzing hair as Jean's voice mail picked up. She remembered what her sister said before this trip, Francie's third to Seattle. Jean loaded her up with condoms and said, *This is it. Six months in, third visit. This is where you get in or get out.* Francie said into the phone, "I'm getting out. I can't get out of the Pacific Northwest fast enough." She wanted to smoke so badly that she started coughing. She stuck a strap of her backpack in her mouth and bit down hard.

A man in a wheelchair stopped at a bench a few feet from her. He was an older man, maybe in his fifties, with silvery hair down to his shoulders and a Fu Manchu mustache. His left leg was missing from the midthigh down, and his blue sweatpants were folded under the stump. He held his left arm close to his body, maneuvering the chair with his right. He carried a duffel bag in his lap and wore a Teva sandal on his good foot. Francie could see his yellow, overgrown toenails, and this made her morning coffee rise in her throat. He did not look in her direction. He repositioned the wheelchair in awkward jerks next to the bench and set the brake. He pulled a cigarette from his shirt pocket and lit it.

Francie rubbed at the goose bumps on her arms and watched the man smoke. She had long noted how people smoked, believing you could tell a lot about their personalities, even how they made love. The man blew the smoke downward. Flicked the ash rather than tapped it. She would say he was thoughtful, calm, occasionally aggressive. She was trying to picture him making love—lying back against the pillows, holding a waist, a breast with one hand. Could he be on top? Could he feel his missing leg? An image of her and Clive came unbidden into her head, a morning of whispers and gentle sweat and blue light.

"Rat fucker," she said, pushing her sunglasses up her nose. "Aldous Huxley meets Atticus Finch *my ass*." The man in the wheelchair did not glance at her, but a woman coming out the doors gave her a look and walked a wide circle around her.

She took a deep breath and hunted in her backpack for nicotine gum. All she found was a restaurant mint at the bottom of the pocket. She picked off the fuzz and popped the mint in her mouth, crunching down hard. She had started smoking when she was fourteen, sneaking Marlboros at the bus stop with her friends, the smoke blending with the puffs of their winter-white breath. That was part of the reason she had quit—after twenty years, her voice was sounding as deep and dry as an old well in the mornings. Aside from the nicotine, she missed the physicality of it, the hot smoke in her lungs, the loose, moist tobacco in the packet. She had picked up rolling to save money, but it also gave her a strange sense of achievement—a tight, neat cigarette, no bulges—and she was tough and wizened and glamorous when she held one loose between her fingers—Greta Garbo meets Madeleine Albright. Without such a prop, she was more of a foul-mouthed, aging woman in a tight tube dress, showing all her dimpled flesh to the world, tugging at the ill-fitting elastic of her life.

The other reason she had quit was because of the nonsmoking Clive. She looked at her hands. She had started picking her cuticles, and her red-rimmed fingernails were tinged blue with cold.

She walked over to the man in the wheelchair. "Excuse me," she said. He looked up at her then. His eyes were large and bright blue, his mustache darker than his hair, and she realized that he was younger than she thought, somewhere in his forties.

She said, "I was wondering, do you think I could bum a cigarette from you?"

He studied her for a moment, or maybe he was looking at his own reflection in her sunglasses. He looked back to the street.

"No," he said.

Francie stood still, her mouth open. In all her years as a smoker, no one had ever said no. *I'm out* maybe, or *It's my last one,* but never *No.*

"Well, do you think I could buy one then?" She felt in her pocket for change. She had stuck some dollar bills in there for airport tips.

"No."

"A dollar." She held it up. "For one smoke."

"Go buy a pack."

"I don't want a pack. I just want one." She could hear her voice, wobbly as a toddler. "Look, I'm kind of having a bad day."

"That's your problem."

Her mouth dropped open all the way. Her throat seized up on her, and she walked back toward her bench. She picked up her old red backpack and started down the stretch of sidewalk, casing the ashtrays for butts, but the sand on each was as raked and clean as a church driveway. A bus from a hotel pulled up. People poured out, arms full of windbreakers and purses and carry-ons. They bustled past, some of them frowning at Francie, who had sat back down on her bench and begun to cry. Big, breaking, shoulder-jerking sobs.

The man in the wheelchair said, "Jesus, lady. Is this what you do when you don't get your way?"

"You know, I am a nice person. I am not mean," she said, plugged-nosed. "I always gave people smokes. Always."

"Good for you."

She shook her head, searching for the words, and all that came out was, "Go to hell."

"Already there." He nodded a couple of times.

"You know, I am this close here." She held up her thumb and index finger. "I'm hanging on by this much."

"Welcome to my world." He took a last drag and flipped his cigarette butt into the street. He popped his jaw for a perfect smoke ring. He said, "Life's a bitch, ain't it?" He lifted his hand in salute.

Francie's hands started to shake. She pushed herself off the bench and stood over him, shoving her sunglasses on top of her head. Her face and neck felt hot, and she knew her eyes were red and puffy. He squinted, folding his good arm across his stomach. His cigarette pack poked out from the top of his shirt pocket. Before he knew what she was doing, she grabbed the pack and stepped backward.

"Why, thank you for your generosity," she said. "Sure, I would *love* a cigarette. How kind of you to ask." She put one in the corner of her mouth. She patted her pockets.

She looked toward the street where he'd tossed his butt, but it had burned out. She looked up and down the stretch of benches, and not one other person was smoking.

"Where are all the goddamn smokers?" she said, the unlit cigarette dangling out of her mouth.

"This is Seattle," the man said. He held up his lighter. He pushed it under the waistband of his sweatpants and snapped the elastic. Then, he *smiled*.

Francie screamed. It was loud enough that it echoed off the concrete terminal, loud enough that her vocal chords burned, loud enough that a security guard headed in their direction and a cabbie driving past flinched and swerved.

The guard looked at the man and then at Francie. "Everything all right?"

Francie nodded. "I was just startled. The wind blew, and something hit me."

The guard frowned.

She said, "I thought it was a bat."

"Bats in the belfry," the man in the wheelchair said.

Francie jerked her thumb at the man. "Painkillers," she whispered loudly to the guard.

The guard gave a slow nod, still frowning, and walked back toward his post.

Francie touched her throat, shivering. She looked at the man in the wheelchair, and he looked back. She crumpled the cigarette in her hand and tore open the top of his pack, dumping the remaining cigarettes onto the sidewalk. She stepped on them, twisting her sneaker on each one. Her sunglasses fell off her head, cracking on the cement, so she stepped on them too until she had created a rather large mess of paper and tobacco and plastic in the middle of the sidewalk.

The man pushed out his cheek with his tongue and sniffed. "You owe me a pack."

"Yeah?" She pointed at his leg. "Make me."

He shook his head and looked back toward the street.

Francie crossed her arms. She said, "Does nothing faze you? Anything at all?"

"Not much. Definitely not temper tantrums or a pint-sized lunatic with hair the color of turnips."

She touched her hair, smoothed down the sides. "You are a wretched little man."

"So I'm told."

Francie checked her watch. It had been only fifteen minutes since the shuttle had dropped her off. Out of the corner of her eye, she saw the guard headed in their direction again. She scooped up the mess on the sidewalk and dumped it in the garbage can. She grabbed her backpack and hurried through the automatic doors into the terminal, thinking of a stop-smoking commercial: A craving lasts only ninety seconds—take a walk!

"Ha!" she said. She wove through the foot traffic, which was growing thicker, people getting out of town early on Friday. She dodged a family that was lumbering past with two strollers, and she ducked into a newsstand. She picked up two chocolate bars, a pack of gum, a lighter, a long-sleeved Mariners T-shirt, a tiger-striped scarf, and a *Sleepless in Seattle* sleep mask, dumping it all at the checkout counter.

"I need a pack of Winstons," she told the clerk. "Actually, two packs."

The clerk started ringing her up. Francie added another candy bar and a cheap pair of sunglasses to the pile. She told the clerk, "I was dumped today. By a man I met on the *Internet*."

The clerk glanced at her but then stared at the register. "That'll be ninety-seven fifty-three," she said.

Francie handed over her credit card, undid her overalls, and pulled the long-sleeved shirt on. The radio was on in the shop, and it was then that Francie learned that Johnny Cash had died that day after a long illness, mere months after his wife, June Carter, had passed away. This news made Francie's throat tighten up again, and she tucked her chin inside her new shirt. She put on the sunglasses, the tag still dangling from the side, wrapped the scarf around her neck, and stuffed the rest of her purchases inside the pockets of her overalls until she bulged like a scarecrow. She unwrapped one of the packs and put a cigarette in the corner of her mouth.

She walked back through the terminal, the unlit cigarette dangling from her mouth, lighter in her hand. She passed a coffee kiosk and realized it was the same one where she had met Clive in person for the first time. They had been phoning and emailing like mad. Once she had gotten past the initial horror of writing to a stranger who had a digital picture of her head, she found that it suited her. She wrote about things she never voiced, like why she had left academia, how it felt like existing in a vacuum, the push-around-the-floor, suck-up-the-hairballs kind. Francie's unfinished dissertation was on hairstyles in the twentieth century, which was how she got into the hair business: field research. At the salon, she got to listen to people talk about the ins and outs of their lives, the births, deaths, work, houses, music, recipes, baseball games, breakups, first dates, weddings, lifetime loves. It was a powerful position, too—people don't mess with you when you're wielding scissors and bleach. Her cyber self was bolder, wittier, sexier—Ani DiFranco meets Clara Bow—than the self who had started to chastise teenage drivers, who talked to herself in public, who woke up alone each morning with ever-lingering creases in her cheeks.

Clive was a Web designer who had majored in history. He read books, played the trumpet, could hold conversations on postmodern criticism and *The Simpsons*, and made Francie laugh hard enough that she tripped over curbs. She had flown to him each time, letting him pay for a hotel. When they first met at the coffee stand, they had stood a couple of feet apart, smiling and staring at each other. He was thinner and taller than Francie had imagined, his dark-brown hair longer than in his pictures, shaggy on his pale forehead and neck. He had stepped forward and put his hand on her face. Later, he had put his hands in her then-blonde hair, kissing her neck and everywhere else he had promised, and she had felt old and new things, naked and trembling.

That morning, Clive had sat across from her on the hotel

bed after they had made love for two days, saying things that she'd heard in other places, at other times, in different terms, from different mouths. *It's not you. It's complicated. I love you, but I can't.* She'd looked at his face—a stranger's face still, though she'd tried to convince herself otherwise—and the pain of past failures had swelled inside her, rising too fast, until she had found it hard to breathe.

Flicking the lighter until the metal was hot, she walked fast through the terminal. She tried to focus on the other, larger things going on in the world at that time: a war in Iraq, soldiers dying every day; Mars glowing orange in the southern sky each night; Johnny Cash gone; the Cubs *and* the Red Sox with shots at making the play-offs. She felt the moments of the world and her world colliding, carved into her as if she were an old park bench.

As soon as she was outside the terminal, Francie cupped her hand and lit the cigarette. Her nostrils flared and she inhaled deeply. The smoke tasted stale and flat, harsh in the back of her throat. She flinched and blew out hard. She took another drag, sucking until the cotton filter was hot, until her cheeks sucked in.

The man in the wheelchair was still sitting in the same place. Francie walked over and sat on the bench next to him.

He looked at her, and she blew a stream of smoke in his face.

"So," she said. "How 'bout those Cubs?"

He glared at her. "I'm a White Sox fan."

"Of course you are." She flicked the cigarette too hard, and the whole cherry fell off. She relit it, wincing at the smoke in her eyes. She pushed her new sunglasses on top of her head. "I don't get you."

"You don't *know* me. Go tell it to someone else."

"A person needs a little help, a little compassion, but not your problem."

"I'm serious, lady." He flicked his wrist. "Get the hell away from me."

She crushed the cigarette under her shoe. She walked behind

him, her head fuzzy with nicotine and lack of sleep. She took off her new scarf, bent down, and wove it through the slats of the wheels and the metal frame under the seat, knotting it tight. She sat back down.

He reached down, grunting, and pulled at the scarf. "Undo it. Now."

"Nope. Not until you say something nice."

He glanced at the security guard, who was pacing about a hundred feet from them.

Francie said, "You could ask that guy for help."

She lit another cigarette, and they stared at each other, smoke curling between them. Francie looked at the man's gray hair.

"I'll start. You have very nice hair. It's in good condition." She studied his head. "Hair has serious roots in social perceptions of sexuality. And race. And power. And politics, of course. It's complex stuff." She reached out to touch it, but he swatted at her hand.

She tapped her ash and blew smoke out of her nose. It tasted terrible, and she was still tense, her stomach hollow and acidy.

"I just found out Johnny Cash died," she said. "I knew it wouldn't be long. When June died, I knew it."

"Or because he spent most of his life as an alcoholic speed freak," the man said.

"You can mess with me, but come on. Johnny Cash."

"Cry me a river." He reached down again, flailing, breathing hard. His armpits were damp.

She said, "I'll help you if you ask me."

"Don't you have a plane to catch?"

She checked her watch. She still had two hours.

He tipped his head back. Francie unwrapped a candy bar and took a bite. They sat for a few moments like that, the man looking up, Francie chewing.

"I have trouble relating to people," Francie said, her mouth full.

"Really. I wouldn't have guessed that."

"I don't generally run around tormenting old men."

He narrowed his eyes. "I'm forty-eight."

"Really. I wouldn't have guessed that." She folded the foil over her chocolate and looked out at the sky. The clouds were moving fast. She wondered where Mars was now. It was even larger here in the thin northern sky. Two nights ago, she and Clive had sat on the hotel balcony, staring up at it. Everything had seemed calm and right and luminous underneath that orange glow. She'd looked at Clive's shadowed profile and thought, Maybe.

She told the man, "Maybe it's some kind of strange energy from Mars throwing things off. It's as close as ever to Earth right now."

"Mars would explain a lot about you."

"You should talk. Fu Manchu meets Bartleby, the Scrivener." She waved her hand, smiling.

He didn't smile back. "What do you want from me? I can't fix anything. I'm just a guy at the airport. I'm just waiting for a ride."

"I don't know. A little compassion. A little interest in a fellow human being."

"That's rich, considering you haven't asked one thing about me." He patted his empty pocket and ran his hand over his head. "Not even, 'What happened to your leg?' Everyone asks that, even if they don't give a goddamn."

Francie looked at his stump, then at the good leg, the yellow toenails. "What happened to your leg?"

He snorted.

She leaned over and held out her half-smoked cigarette. He hesitated a moment but took it.

"What happened?"

"None of your business." He took a couple of deep drags. He said, "Vietnam."

"I'm sorry."

He nodded. He lifted his hand and looked at the cigarette. He said, "June wrote 'Ring of Fire.'" He glanced at her. "June Carter wrote 'Ring of Fire,' not Johnny."

"I know."

"So, that's something nice."

"That's stating a fact. If you would've said, 'June and Johnny were an honest-to-God love story,' you'd be a free man."

He let out a disgusted sigh. He narrowed his eyes at her. "What's that hair color?"

"It's black cherry."

"You did that on purpose?"

"Hey."

"It doesn't suit you." He looked at her head, at her face, and down her body. Her stomach gave a slight jump, and she thought again of him lying on his back and what it would feel like on top of him. Her cheeks grew hot.

He said, "You should grow it out."

"Don't be so predictable. I look terrible in long hair. My face is too long and oval for it."

"Your face is fine."

"Clive liked my short hair." She touched the edges, remembering his hands and breath on her neck. "Although, he did say 'Whoa' when he saw the color."

He raised an eyebrow.

She shrugged. "A man I was dating. Someone who won't be writing me a love song." She touched the tip of her cold nose, and the smell of cigarettes on her fingers made her flinch. "Things haven't been going very well."

"You can't always make people behave the way you want them to."

"I didn't mean him. I meant me. But that's quite an assumption. I didn't try to make him 'behave' in any way." She pushed her cold hands between her knees. "It's really not about him. It's more like an amalgamation of things. But it's true that he doesn't love me."

"I hope you're not asking me to feel sorry for you."

"God, no. Not *empathy*. Never that." Francie exhaled hard.

"You're not a woman, that's for sure. A woman would have said, 'It's not you, honey.' Even if it wasn't true."

"Clearly, I am not a damn woman."

Francie felt a tightness in her lungs, her mouth dry and tinny. That pain was rising again, glass shards in her veins. She looked at her hands, at the inflamed cuticles, the wrinkles and dry skin, the dirt and chocolate under the fingernails. She stood and walked behind the man. She leaned down, untied the scarf, and put her face next to his. His mustache brushed her cheek, and his long hair was soft on her ear. She smelled laundry soap and cigarettes and sweat.

She said, "I want you to tell me something good. Something. Lie if you have to. Or you are going off that curb." At that moment, she meant it. A shaking, blind anger radiated off her skin and got trapped in her clothes, a hot smell of nicotine and iron and talc. She put her knee against the chair and gave it a shove. He was heavier than she'd thought. She shoved it again, harder. He put his foot down and held out his hand.

She pushed him forward until the wheels were a few inches from the curb and then rolled him back. "It's not that high. Maybe you wouldn't get that hurt. Unless I get some momentum." She took another step back.

He cleared his throat but didn't say anything.

Francie glanced at the security guard, who was talking to someone in a car. The man touched his temple, pushed at his hair. She watched his belly rise and fall.

"Afraid?" she said into his ear. "Welcome to my world."

He scratched at a spot on his stump. Francie leaned forward, angling her body so that she could see his face. He licked his lips and looked her in the eye. She was close enough to see the different colors in his mustache and eyebrows.

He said, "Go for it."

He lifted his foot and faced the street. He gripped the chair with his good arm.

"Do it," he said. "Do it."

Francie looked at the back of the man's head, at his shiny, healthy hair, again at a loss for words. She turned her head away. She was so tired and ashamed that she sat down on the concrete. Her sunglasses slipped down her nose. She sat with her hand over her mouth, her left leg growing wet from a puddle.

"Okay," she said. "Okay."

She untied the scarf, put it around her neck, and stood up, brushing at the dampness on her pants. She adjusted her sunglasses and checked her watch. Hefting up her backpack, she pulled both cigarette packs from her pocket. She tossed them in his lap.

He put the packs in his shirt pocket. He nodded at her, and she nodded back. She walked toward the doors. Her backpack slipped, and she hefted it up higher.

"Hey," the man called out.

Francie looked back at him.

He said, "It's not you, honey." He didn't smile, but he held up his hand. He wheeled himself down the sidewalk.

Francie watched him go, the second man who had made her cry that day. She wiped under her eyes and blew into her cold hands, rubbing them together. She went through security and waited in a plastic chair, her red pack on the seat next to her. Passengers emerged from the tunnels, dazed, rumpled, towing cargo and kids. How quickly things could change. Just like that, for better or worse. She checked her watch—still more than an hour until her flight. She looked at her boarding pass, her ticket out of that city. The date was bold and black: September 12, 2003. The day she got dumped. The day she accosted a man in a wheelchair. The day she quit smoking, again. The jagged day that she already wanted like hell to forget. She sat at the terminal, and she closed her eyes, willing it all to hurry up and fade, as if by sheer resolve she could hasten the process, do without the weeks of hollow nights and red eyes, so that tomorrow she would wake up with shoulder-length hair the color of topaz, her mind on something else, and that old lousy day would come to her as she stepped off a curb somewhere, the faces now nothing but flashes of light, the details muted fragments: the flick of a lighter, the glow of a planet, the soft hair of a stranger, an old self who struggled with the new, who loved and lost, who wore sunglasses in the rain.

All This History at Once

Stairs. Steep, slippery, marble sons-of-bitches, wide as a ranch house. As you lug your booth supplies up the steps to the Tennessee capitol plaza, you don't have to look back to feel the fall. A hollow, looping kind of vertigo, a fizzy pressure in your ears. It happens every time you tackle a flight of stairs like this one, or worn shag carpet, or tile or hardwood or pebbled concrete with gaps the size of small dogs. God forbid if you're wooly from allergy meds or sleep-deprived because of your daughter's tonsillitis or your husband's snoring or your persistent bouts of insomnia. Or like today, if you're wearing the red cowboy boots that you pulled from the back of the closet instead of your usual sturdy, rubber-soled canvas slip-ons, good for middle school art classrooms or chasing three-year-olds around the yard. On impulse, you also had packed a midthigh denim skirt and a filmy boatneck top, which this morning you paired with the slick-soled boots, a decision that you regret now as you do a sideways, elderly shuffle up the stairs, conscious of your knees, where the skin is giving in to gravity. Elephant knees. Not to mention, your inner thighs are rubbing together. You've got enough friction down there to ignite a rocket.

But you're here this weekend, after all, for an arts and crafts festival, where red cowboy boots and short skirts are de rigueur, and with any luck, no children will puke or pee on you or smear you with paste or peanut butter or grape-scented markers. Your daughter is back in central Phoenix with your mother-in-law, playing with her cousins and wood blocks and later going to the state fair, where she will certainly puke or pee on your mother-in-law and possibly strangers. Today, you're a grown-up again, a thousand miles from home at one of the country's premier arts and crafts festivals on the grounds of Tennessee's historic capitol. You and your husband are selling your whimsical wooden mailboxes and wind chimes. Your husband's wicked with a lathe and jigsaw, a skill he hones on weekends, a reprieve from teaching twitchy middle schoolers about the earth's crust and the periodic table. You design the boxes and cutouts, he builds them, you paint them, quite the little operation out there in the workshop he built in your central Phoenix backyard. You're back in the art game. Sort of. Used to be you sold linocuts and lithographs to galleries, work that you long ago bundled up in cardboard tubes and stuffed into the attic. Different art, different life, that.

Today, aside from the inner-thigh situation, things are going lovely—you sold the vw bus mailbox and the Roseanne Roseannadanna wind chime, and damn if it isn't a gorgeous, sunny day—until you spot your ex-husband, whom you haven't seen in more than three years, four booths down. There he is, down the yawning corridor between all those squinty folks fondling silver rings and scarves, his gray tufts sticking on end like a potted plant. There he is, selling his raku bowls and mugs and shapely freestanding sinks. You didn't know he'd be here. You didn't know if he was making art anymore—you haven't seen him at this festival in two years, and the last time you checked his university website, he was on leave. You weren't sure, frankly, where he was. There he is.

Your husband—the present one, the father of your child—sees him too. The silence balloons inside your booth, a big plastic globe of a moment. He hooks his thumbs into the belt loops of his jeans, those callused hands that you love, hands steady at the saw, at the wheel, on you. When he's upset, he clenches up and somehow looks even lower to the ground. In college, he'd been an all-star catcher, could block runners twice his size from the plate, squat for hours on those thick legs. He knows the story, of course, that the ex was your professor, older by fifteen years and married at the time you met, the whole soap-operatic mess stretching into the better part of a decade for what should have lasted a year, tops. Of course he knows. He was there, after all, sharing what seemed like a thousand Styrofoam cups of bad coffee in the teachers' lounge, letting you talk if you wanted, or not, or bawl your brains out on occasion, handing you clumps of brown paper towels to snuffle into. He was waiting for you when you finally walked out the door, and you were pregnant before the ink dried on the divorce papers. Still, you say to him now: Honey, that ship sailed years ago. He's not a bad person. It wasn't like that. Whose life turns out like they wanted, anyway? As soon as you say it, his brows lock together, and he hunkers down another inch or two. You say, Shit. You tell him you didn't mean it like that. You love *him*. You don't want this to turn into something. You'll get lemonades, okay? You'll be right back. You grab your purse and hurry off. You don't give him a chance to ask what you are thinking: Why *are* you wearing that skirt, Odette?

You keep your head down when you pass the ex-husband's booth, trying to quell the spasm that seems to be traveling from stomach to intestine. There's a crowd around his booth, so maybe he doesn't see you. As you scurry beyond his booth, beyond the peddlers of tin angels and knitted doll babies and decoupage bottle caps, you think of what you don't tell your steady, all-star catcher of a husband: the ex still turns up in your dreams some nights. Don't go, he says. Stay. Sometimes, when he asks in these dreams of yours, you do. You curl up next to him on the futon. He smells of trash-can fires and clay. He still burns, this man. But the fact is, in the waking world, in those long days when he sank into his futon or locked himself in his studio or disappeared for days, he never asked. And you left, saving yourself instead of him.

You crab-walk up another set of steps that stretch the length of a swimming pool, the marble worn smooth by years of rain and legislators and Civil War foot soldiers. Today, a sunny and warm Saturday in early October, the steps have become bleachers, a shady resting spot for festivalgoers who gnaw sausages-on-sticks and candy apples and fistfuls of kettle corn. At the top is a frozen-lemonade stand. You will grab those treats for you and your husband, but first you duck into the restroom to rub a damp paper towel on your poor old chafing thighs. In the restroom, you splash water on your cheeks. You stand as tall as you can. You jimmy your bra, give your breasts a heave, try to make them stay *up*. You suck it in.

At the top of the steps, your hands full of lemonade, you lean on an Ionic column to take in the view, the alien bumpy horizon of trees and buildings, a few snitches of yellow in the green leaves. Back home, it's still sweltering in the hundreds, but here, a sturdy breeze whips the flags atop the famed capitol cupola. Somewhere down there are the ornate bronzed Andrew Jackson statue and James K. Polk's tomb. All this history at once. You breathe deep and look down, scouting the booths. With the drinks melting fast in your hands and your eyes on the two loves of your life down there—one present, one past—you step out. The chunky, slick heel of that red boot catches, and your left ankle, which never healed right from the time you sprained it twenty-five years ago getting off the Tilt-A-Whirl at the state fair, gives way. And this time, you go down.

It's funny how the mind works. In the million times you've imagined this, you were sure that you'd think about the humiliation—your skirt rucked up, revealing all the dimpled flesh, the drumstick thighs, the striped cotton briefs that have seen better days but sure are comfortable on your ever-spreading hips. You'd hear bystanders trying to hold in hysterical snorts and snickers as if they were in church. You'd worry about your head, your elbows, the knees, those fragile exposed parts—osteoporosis, for God's sake! You haven't had a glass of milk in twenty years.

You were sure your life would flash before you in some way. The choices you've made in this short, tumbling life would become clear, as if you could see them, magnified, holistic. The clarity of the doomed. Maybe your daughter on the swing set, shouting, Higher, Mama! Higher! Or your husband, the present one, sleeping on his side in the cot next to you after your daughter is born, the vulnerable, unshaven line of his jaw, his short legs pulled up to his chest. Or your husband, the past one, staring out the window, not looking at you even when you leaned over the futon and waved your hand in front of his face. You'd see yourself laying out the do-it-yourself divorce kit on the kitchen table, the little orange sticky tabs carefully attached: sign here, and here, and here. Your litho stone in the yard where you dropped it from shoulder height, cracked, unusable, because the art in you had shriveled up like dead skin. In this bright flashing moment, you'd know if you were right to leave, to choose a new life. If you deserved such a thing.

But no, no flashes. Nothing flashes before you except the last blinding glimpse of a donkey-shaped Mylar balloon bouncing in the wind above the rows of white-tented booths, the glint of sun off a jet wing. Nothing. You just fall.

You don't stop at a few steps—oh no, you go all the way down. Your frozen lemonades go flying, spraying you and some of the other unfortunate step-sitters with sticky flecks of ice. Your purse explodes and spills out its entrails of tampons and receipts and spare change and mints, tick tick tick as they roll and scatter. Tumble, bump, oof, pell-mell, all striped grandma underpants and thigh flab, whoopsie-fucking-daisy, your red-booted feet wheeling like a carnival ride. Twenty-two steps later, you land stunningly upright on your backside, spread-eagled, at the bottom.

You can't get up. Your right forearm pulses with pain, the wrist bones already lost inside the puffed-up skin, and your damn left ankle is going to swell to the size of a grapefruit inside that boot. You'll be finding new bruises for weeks, which your daughter will count and trace as though part of a collection. You're going to need some help here. And look, people are running to you, not a laughing face among them. They're all pulled-down eyebrows and O mouths. There's the lady with the zebra hat, the Elvis impersonator, the kettle corn peddler. There's your husband, the present one, all eye-popping panic and sweet Jesuses and honey baby sweethearts. The past husband isn't there. Of course he isn't. He never was, never ever, was he?

You're on the ground, swelling in all kinds of places. The sun is shining down hard. The cement hot on your exposed thighs, you rock yourself a little, feeling the heat, and now the pain, rising. But there's something else too, coming up fast. It burns and bursts forth with a carbonated sting: a laugh. You're laughing. You're doubled over by it, gales of effervescent, stomach-clenching glee. Because you're alive. What's more, you're the lady at the arts festival who fell down the capitol steps. That's *you*. What a goddamn spectacle. You want to draw it, etch it into a zinc plate or carve it into wood. You hope to God that someone got it on tape.

You laugh until the tears are streaming down, until your face is tracked with mascara and snot, until spit strings out from your bottom lip. You hold up a finger to your kneeling husband (Look at him. There he is. And how'd you pull that off, you silly, lucky, skirt-wearing woman?) to tell him you're all right. You really are. You need just another minute. Just a minute, if that's all right. Really, you're fine.

Fossil Light

The vow of silence was Faith's idea. A week after her birthday party she came home, threw her keys on the sofa, and stood with her arms crossed in front of the television until Denny turned it off.

"Here it is," she said. "I figure since we're not speaking anyway, we should make it count. We'll be like the monks."

"What monks?" he said.

"I don't know what monks," she said. "The ones in a monastery somewhere. They don't speak to each other. They concentrate and pray and meditate. They ask for miracles." She wiped at beads of perspiration on her nose. Faith had always been sweaty, and Denny knew that she was embarrassed by it. She carried handkerchiefs, surreptitious bits of color tucked in pockets and purses that she pulled out like a magician. She drew out a magenta one and dabbed her face.

Denny sighed and put his big hands on his knees. He had been sleeping in the spare room, his feet hanging off the end of the hide-a-bed. Faith and Edgar had stayed at her parents' for a couple of days after the party, and the boy was still stay-ing with them.

"I know I messed up," Denny said. "I know it. It was an awful thing to do, and I don't think I can say how sorry I am, though I want to try. Maybe we should try talking first."

"I can't talk to you," she said.

He stood and walked over to her. He wanted to tell her about the money he'd been saving, his father's old tools that he'd been selling off from what his mother had left him when she'd moved in with her new husband, the cash that *her* mother had been slipping him at Sunday dinners. He had a job interview. He was turning a corner here. He was going to do better.

But Faith stepped back and put her hand up. "I've been think-ing about this. I mean it."

"Okay," he said. "Tell me."

"No talking," she said. "No sound. No words inside this house."

"What about notes?"

"No notes."

"Even deaf people get notes," he said.

"We're not deaf."

"Faith, come on. I don't know what else to do. I don't know what I can say except I'm sorry. I feel awful. Nothing like that will ever happen again. It won't. And I'm going to get another job. I have an interview Thursday at a newspaper press room." He rubbed his hands on his knees, feeling the rough denim. "I am trying. I know you *never* screw up—"

She gave a short laugh. "Don't put this on me. This isn't about me." She threw up her hands. "This is what I'm saying. I can't talk to you."

"Please," he said.

She frowned and bit her thumbnail. "No sound."

"For how long?"

"I don't know." She shrugged. "Mom said Edgar can stay with

them for a few days. He's fine, you know, in case you were wondering at all."

He looked at his hands. "I am trying, Faith."

Faith sighed. "He's fine. Happy school's out. They're taking him to a baseball game tomorrow."

"They hate me, too, I suppose."

She looked at the floor. "No one hates you, Denny."

He rubbed the back of his neck. "When do we start?"

She drew her finger across her lips and threw away the key. She nodded, walked to their bedroom, and shut the door.

*

The first full day of silence began on a Wednesday. The house was quiet except for the muffled city noise outside—fan belts squawked, tires screeched, loose hubcaps rattled. Denny, Faith, and their son lived in a one-story brick house that used to be a jewelry store. It was off Seventh Avenue, a stretch of road north of the downtown Phoenix skyscrapers, the same neighborhood where Denny grew up. Industrial shops blended with apartments, antique shops, drive-thru liquor stores, and empty lots, always shifting. In a span of months, places like Johnny's Used Work Uniforms became a Mexican pottery outlet, a transmission shop became a purveyor of wicker furniture, and Madame Beulah's Precious Gems became Faith and Denny's home. Though Faith had grown up in the suburbs, where large homes with putting-green lawns and matching stucco sprawled on the sunny hillsides like spoiled teenagers, she liked this part of the city better, the old, tree-lined neighborhoods and the bedroom view of Camelback Mountain to the east. She liked what she called the neighborhood's temperamental nature, its potential. Denny didn't see it this way. He saw it as the area he'd wanted to get out of. He saw the peeling paint and scrubby lots, the onslaught of billboards around them. The windows had bars on them, and the evaporative cooler leaked—the ceiling in Edgar's room had a brown stain that Faith liked to say was the shape of Florida. But, Denny knew, they could afford the rent. And that was his fault.

Faith came into the guest room before sunrise, lean as a wire hanger in the blue-gray morning. Denny watched from the guest bed as she stood at the closet in her slip. She'd lost weight—too much—and he could see the curved lines of her ribs. As she pulled a blouse and skirt from the closet, she saw Denny watching her. She always said that the reason she fell in love with Denny was because of how he looked at her, from the first time she glanced back and caught him watching her walk away from a restaurant table, his chin in his palm. He joked it off, saying, Who wouldn't watch that ass? What he didn't say was that it was because he couldn't shake the feeling that she might not come back. Even when she was pregnant, he could picture her climbing out the bathroom window and catching a cab to a place that he would never find.

The first time he saw her was at a party near the community college where they both had been students, he taking basic math and biology toward his dream of studying astronomy. She had been leaning against the wall, all teased white-gold hair and eyeliner and lusty hips. He was a big young man, a good foot and a half taller than her and, at eighteen, still growing into his large pale hands and feet. When he caught her eye, she jutted her chin, cracking her gum, and stared him down. Later, she pickpocketed his wallet, took the cash, and called him the next day to tell him she found it. She still picked pockets sometimes now when she was nervous or upset, or if some customer pissed her off, especially the rich ones. She took the money, left the cards, and gave the money to charity. It was one of the first things he loved about her, a girl who stole for good.

Faith sat down on the edge of the bed. Denny pulled the covers up under his chin, his feet sticking out from the blanket. She fiddled with the dress clothes in her lap. Denny knew that she liked wearing those clothes—the wispy, efficient sound of panty-hose against her skirts, the button at the base of her throat, the ironed cloth at her wrists, all light-years from past waitressing aprons or wrinkled cotton smudged by little-boy hands, from the old rebellious days when she picked pockets and slept with young men like Denny for sport.

That Wednesday morning of silence, he did the same thing as the first time he saw her at that college party six years ago.

He held up his hand. *Hi.*

She held hers up too. *Hi yourself.*

*

On Wednesday night, Denny watched soundless TV with captioning while Faith worked on a crossword puzzle. Denny channel-surfed until he found a special about supernovas, about a discovery that the universe was accelerating, expanding at a faster and faster rate because of something called dark energy.

"Wow," Denny said, and Faith shook her pen at him. He gestured at the TV and tapped his forehead. *Watch this. This is mind-blowing.*

She turned back to her puzzle.

Denny frowned. The first time he told Faith about wanting to be an astronomer, back when they first met and spent most of their afternoons in bed, she had laughed. And I'm the pope, she'd said, laughing some more, her freckled shoulders shaking under the bed covers, until she saw his face. She said, Hell, Denny, I'm sorry, I didn't know you meant it. She stripped the covers down to her waist, showing all her plump flesh and dark freckles. Connect the dots, she said, grabbing his hand. Show me some constellations.

The TV captioning said that light from exploding stars held answers to the mysterious energy. It was called fossil light. Denny smiled. He had learned about fossil light in grade school when he'd gone on a field trip to the science museum. It was one of his favorite things, that light through space was not the same age as light on earth. That with telescopes you could see light from when the universe began. He'd run home from the bus stop that day, his lunch pail banging his knee, to tell his mother. His mother was at the sink, peeling potatoes, when he burst into the kitchen. His father was gone by then. Mom, guess what? I'm gonna be an astronomer, he told her. I'm gonna discover new planets and stars. She didn't turn around. She kept peeling, the brown skins piled high. That's nice, honey, she said. That's real good. Denny told her he wanted to get a telescope, that he'd name a star for her and maybe his brother, and he was so busy talking that he didn't notice his mother crying until she set down the peeler and slid down against the cupboards. He pulled at her hands, and she held his hand to her cheek, sticky with starch. You're just a little boy, she said.

Denny turned to his wife. He wanted to tell her this. He sat down across from her. There were two wallets on the table near her elbow. He reached over her and tapped the wallets, raising his eyebrows. She shrugged and hunched over her crossword. He picked up her wrist and began to trace a pattern of four freckles. She mouthed, *Ganymede, Calisto, Io, Europa.* Jupiter's moons. She remembered.

He leaned forward and kissed the inside of her wrist, and she pulled back. She folded her hands in her lap. She shook her head, her eyes on the table. She could have been thinking a lot of things—I don't know, Not yet, I'm confused, It's not that easy, I'm not ready—but this is what Denny understood: *How could you? He's just a little boy. That night. I won't ever forgive you for that. How could you?*

Faith doodled stars on the edge of the newspaper. He took the pen from her. Next to the stars he wrote, *It wasn't me.* She frowned and tilted her head. But Denny didn't know how to explain what he meant, either with or without words. He did not look at her before he pushed back and turned off the television, heading for the guest room.

*

On Thursday morning Denny woke in the dark to get ready for his interview. He hadn't slept well. He crept into the bedroom and kissed Faith on the forehead while she slept. She didn't stir. Sleepy, he stopped in Edgar's room to do the same before remembering the boy wasn't there. He flipped on the light and looked around the room. Faith's parents had bought Edgar a *Star Wars* bedspread, from the new episode, Darth Maul instead of Darth Vader, young Obi-Wan instead of Luke Skywalker. Denny touched the bed and empty pillow. He sat down on the bed and stared up at the stain on the ceiling. He thought of the night of the party.

That night, Denny had gotten home late, the passenger seat full of ice bags. He'd stopped on his way home to pawn his father's jigsaw. In those past two months, he'd saved $300 from the pawn shop and from the money that his mother-in-law had sneaked him. Maybe not life-changing but enough for something, at least enough for a birthday present for his wife, though he hadn't gotten anything yet. He'd been hiding the cash under the car seat in an envelope inside an old cigar box where he also kept a stash of candy to keep Edgar occupied during the rare times the boy rode alone with his father. The ice bags felt good on his arms, chafed from loading boxes all day.

Inside the house, Edgar sat planted in front of a *Star Wars* video and barely took his eyes off the screen to say hi to his father. The kitchen counter was lined with bags of chips and soda and beer cans. Faith stacked cups on the kitchen table. She wore a black dress that cut in a V down her back, black hose with a seam up the back of her leg.

Denny touched Faith's back with the corner of an ice bag, and she jumped. She turned and looked at him, her lips pressed tight.

"There's a message for you on the machine," she said, turning her back to him. "From work."

He put the ice in the freezer and played the machine. His

boss's secretary wanted to know where they should send his last paycheck—Denny hadn't left an address.

Denny rubbed his forehead. "Faith."

Faith grabbed two six-packs of beer off the counter and shoved them into his stomach. "I don't want to hear it," she said.

Denny took the beer and put it in the cooler. The shipping company had been his fifth job in a year, and he'd been there for two months, loading and lifting boxes onto cars bound for places he had never seen—New Haven, White Plains, Des Moines. That morning, he had listened to his coworkers talk about pay raises and their dipshit bosses and getting some pussy over the weekend. Sweat dripped down his back and belly, the cardboard rubbing a rash on his arms. Because he was big, they gave him the big, heavy loads. As trucks pulled away from the loading dock, he'd thought about doing this every day for the rest of his life, lifting, loading, sweating. Like his father, who had come home exhausted and grimy from his work at different auto repair shops until he left when Denny was eight. After his father had a few beers, or as he was washing his hands with industrial orange soap, he'd tell his son, You need to do better than this. Denny hadn't understood at the time, but that morning his throat had constricted to the point that he would not have been able to speak if he'd tried. But he hadn't tried to speak. He'd lifted, loaded, and sweated.

Denny went into the living room. Edgar sat on the floor in front of the TV, his skinny legs bouncing with energy. His son was among the taller kids in the first grade. He had Faith's light hair and dark freckles, which covered both of them like paint spatters. Denny sat behind him on the sofa and put a hand on the boy's head. He remembered himself at that age, when all that mattered was Legos and *Star Wars* and how long until supper was ready. Edgar turned and grinned at him with those big, ridged teeth, a shock of hair in his eyes. Denny smiled. It wasn't that he didn't *like* his son. He had been nineteen when Edgar was born, had known Faith only six months when she got pregnant. He was a boy-man who had never lived on his own, who worked sporadically, who was still more interested in sleeping with his wife than listening to her. It was as if his own half-shaped life had ended when his son's started. Denny the father. Denny the husband. Denny the worker.

As the first party guests arrived, some of Faith's coworkers from the bank, Denny stood in the kitchen in his long sleeves and slacks, his hair still damp from the shower. He grew intensely aware of the razor-wire fence around the empty lot next door, the rust stains in the bathroom sink, the rough calluses on his hands. He checked his fingernails for dirt. He fixed himself a large whiskey and Coke and drank half of it, his throat burning. He looked around the small kitchen, at the fridge covered with photos and Edgar's drawings and awards, at the curtains Faith made to match her hand towels and potholders. She had sewn more for the living room and bedrooms, using bright, remnant-store fabrics to distract from the shabbiness of their belongings.

Denny spent the party gathering up used plates and cups, emptying ashtrays, changing music, and refilling drinks, especially his own. He watched Faith. As the night progressed, Faith's cheeks grew flushed, and her mascara smudged, deepening the shadows under her eyes. When she leaned forward to blow out the candles on her cake, her dress gaped at the front, showing her black bra and sharp collarbones. He wondered what that deep-cut dress would feel like on his skin. Like black spiders, maybe. Like fingertips. She danced with her boss, and when the man left, glassy-eyed, Denny noticed red lipstick on his collar.

By the time everyone had gone and Edgar was long asleep, Denny was very drunk. He and Faith were in the bedroom. He leaned in the doorway, and Faith sat cross-legged on the bed and took her mascara off with lotion on tissues. For a moment, her face looked like a stranger's, a beautiful, tired young woman whom he might flirt with in line at the supermarket.

"Are you sleeping with your boss?" he asked.

Faith looked through her fingers at him. "You have got to be kidding me."

"It's a legitimate question." He didn't believe this was true, but it was something he imagined sometimes when he slept pressed up against her, even when they made love. She would leave, choose someone else.

"This night turned out to be fun, despite everything. So please don't ruin it."

He said, "You don't believe in me."

"You have no moral ground here, Denny. You're the one who doesn't have a job. Again."

"Even if I did, *Faith*, it wouldn't matter. Nothing I do matters to you."

"That is not true." She balled up a tissue and dropped it on the bed.

"No. You don't listen. You don't hear me. Never have."

She squinted at him. "What the hell are you talking about?"

"I embarrass you."

"No. Well, right now you do."

Outside, a police helicopter flew overhead, buzzed in circles, its searchlight flashing against the curtains. Sirens whined and faded, setting off the neighborhood dogs. Denny swayed on his feet and grabbed the doorframe. "Do you love that kid more than me?"

"That kid is your son, Denny."

"Answer the goddamn question."

She shook her hair out of her face and looked up at him. He saw it in her eyes.

Yes.

He took his bottle of beer and poured it over her head, the whole bottle, soaking her hair, her pretty black dress, the bed, the tissues smudged with makeup. It ran in her eyes, her ears, and her mouth and down her back and onto the sheets as she crouched forward and put her head between her knees.

He went across the hall to his son's room. He pulled the little boy out of bed by the front of his pajamas, holding Edgar's sleepy face up to his own.

"What about you?" He shook the boy. "Do you love her more than me?"

Edgar blinked in confusion. "Daddy?"

Denny carried him across the hall, and before Faith could get up, he dropped his son on top of her. Edgar started crying, too, and Denny looked down at both of them.

"Happy birthday," he said.

*

Denny arrived early at his job interview at the press room. The man who was going to interview him was in the middle of a press run, so Denny waited and watched. He sipped a Styrofoam cup of coffee with powdered creamer, trying not to yawn. The press was a roaring, hungry machine that shook the building, and all the workers wore earplugs. The boss pulled paper after paper off the conveyor belt, checking the colors and calling out on a PA system for adjustments. The ink smelled as strong as roofing tar or hot asphalt, and everything was marked with black—the furniture, walls, coffeepot, tables, clothes, skin. The workers all wore cloth booties over their shoes, like at a hospital. Denny checked the soles of his boots, and sure enough, they were smudged with black.

Denny picked up a newspaper on the chair next to him and flipped through it. He stopped on the science page. There was an article about the dark energy discovery that he'd seen on TV the night before. He blinked fast and shook his head, overwhelmed by déjà vu. In that time-elapsed moment, he felt sure he'd been in that room before, staring at the churning, blurred papers that would end up on thousands of driveways and breakfast tables, sure too that he had brushed at his shirt and straightened his collar, hopeful, as the press rolled like thunder beneath his feet.

*

After the interview, Denny stopped by his in-laws' to see Edgar. Faith's mother opened the door. His mother-in-law was a short, steel-haired woman who was kinder than her pinpricked mouth suggested.

"I got a job." He stuck his hands in his pockets. "At a press room. I start tomorrow."

She nodded and opened the door wider. "He's in the office, on the computer." She followed Denny down the hall.

The boy sat at a desk, clicking a mouse, his face too close to the computer screen. Denny knelt beside Edgar's chair. "Hi, Dad," he said without taking his eyes from the screen.

"What're you reading about there?"

"Artificial gravity," Edgar said.

Denny laughed. "What?"

Edgar turned to him, his freckled face upturned, his gray-green eyes serious. He looked so much like Faith that Denny caught his breath.

"Artificial gravity," Edgar said. "You know, for the astronauts. It would really help them."

"Yes, I know, but where did you learn about that?"

Edgar shrugged. "School. The Internet."

Denny stood, his knees cracking. He put his large hands on the boy's head, stroking the smooth white hair. "I think that's a great idea, son," he said. He glanced at Faith's mother, who was still standing in the doorway. She gave a small smile, nodded, and left the room.

As he backed his car out of the driveway, his mother-in-law came out, waving her arms. He rolled down the window, and she leaned in. She pressed a thick fold of twenty-dollar bills into his palm.

She said, "Edgar needs a father. I'm doing this for him. You hear me?"

Denny nodded.

"I know she can be hard on people. I know. But she is my daughter," she said, putting her hand flat over her heart and then on Denny's hand. "Do you understand?"

He nodded again. He pulled the box from underneath the seat and tucked the money inside the envelope in there.

"Please don't mess this up," she said.

*

Denny stopped at the hardware store on his way home, and he got home at dark, loaded down with bags. He found a note from Faith.

So I lied about the notes (ha ha). I have to go to this seminar after work tonight, and then the girls and I are going out for some drinks. I'll probably be late. There's stuff in the fridge. Faith.

Denny brought all the bags into Edgar's room. He covered the floor and bed with old sheets and got a chair from the kitchen. He began to work. He worked until his neck and back cramped and his arms ached. Around midnight, he lay down on Edgar's bed and turned off the light. He surveyed his work. It wasn't bad. It wasn't bad at all.

*

The next morning, he found another note: *Dinner tonight? 6 o'clock. F.* He hadn't gotten a chance to tell her about his new job, which had run late because of the paperwork he had to fill out. By six o'clock he was ten minutes from home. The sun was nearly down for the day, razor-cut clouds across the horizon. He rolled down the window and hooked his arm over the door. Ink smeared his arms and work shirt. His first day had gone well. His boss told him he had an eye for color. Was quick and steady. You could do well here, he said.

Denny was about a mile from his turnoff when the traffic slowed, a mass of taillights flaring red. He pressed his own brakes hard, checking the car behind him. He pictured Faith in the kitchen, her brow furrowed, stirring ground beef for sloppy joes and listening for the car to pull in. He leaned out the window, trying to see the problem. Traffic crept forward until it stopped.

Denny reached for the box under the seat, his eyes on the traffic. He felt around in the box and looked down. The envelope of cash was gone. His heart started to thump hard, his mind racing. Did he take it out, was the car unlocked, where did he put it? He'd been so tired. "Jesus," he said. He started to sweat, looking around to see if anything else was missing. There was nothing to steal except some old tapes and a tire pressure gauge, a newspaper on the seat. He unwrapped a piece of stale taffy and snapped off a piece. He revved the engine. Traffic moved in awkward lurches. He was only a half-mile to the next exit, but it would probably take another fifteen minutes to get to it. The freeway flickered with cars and fading light. He thought about gunning it down the shoulder, past the waiting line, the hot engines, the drivers with their chins on their steering wheels. He unwrapped a piece of gum and chomped it until his jaw ached.

*

Denny turned fast into the carport, the car's tires squealing. He needed to search under the seats for the envelope, but he was forty-five minutes late. When he got inside, the stereo was on, but there were no signs of Faith. He could smell onions and garlic and something else, candle wax maybe. He went from room to room. Their bedroom door was shut. He slid down and sat against it. His shirt was drenched with sweat and ink. He began to knock, panic rising, like the day he woke up after the party and saw that they were gone, and he ran from room to room, checking closets, retching in sinks.

"I'm in here," Faith called out. She was in Edgar's room, stretched out on his bed.

Denny said, "You're talking."

She shrugged. "It was a stupid idea."

"I was stuck in traffic," he said.

"Okay."

"I was."

She lifted her head and looked at him. "Good lord, you're covered in black."

"I got a job at a newspaper press."

"That's right. You said you had an interview." She dropped her head back on the pillow. "I was lying here remembering this boy I knew once from church. He died in this really terrible way when we were kids. It was the strangest thing, though, when I heard he died, it was like I already knew. Somehow I already knew." She pulled out a blue-checkered handkerchief and wiped her nose.

She rolled onto her side. "Tonight, when you didn't show up, I started to work myself into the rage of the century. But then, for some reason, I knew that I was wrong. That you would come and that something else happened, but you were okay. I have no idea how I knew that. But I was lying here and it was like it had all already happened. Like a whopping déjà vu. Maybe it was that thing you used to talk about, about that spooky particle behavior stuff."

"Quantum mechanics," he said.

"Right," she said. "See? I was listening." She blew at her bangs. "I do listen. I do. Like all that stuff you told me once about how the light from the stars is old, light that has already happened. Has it changed by the time it gets here? I don't know."

She sat up and lifted the pillow, pulling out Denny's envelope of cash.

"Where did you get this?" she asked.

He sighed and sat on the edge of the bed. Faith the pickpocket.

"I thought I lost that," he said. "Your mom gave me part of it. I saved the rest."

"How?"

He folded his hands. "My mother's things. Dad's tools."

"Oh, Denny."

"They weren't worth much."

"Still. They were yours. Why?"

"It started out that I wanted to get you something nice for your birthday." He licked his lips. He looked at the ceiling. He pointed at it. "When I was a kid, I wanted to be an astronomer. But I realize it's too late for that."

He half-hoped she would argue, say, No, it's never too late, but he knew that she wouldn't. She touched his arm.

She said, "You're not the only one whose life didn't turn out as planned."

He looked at his wife's fingers on his skin. "It's for Edgar," he said. "For college."

"You should have told me."

He scratched his cheek and looked down at his ink-stained shoes. He thought of his mother slouched against the cupboards, back when the stars were new, galaxies within reach. His father, always washing his always-stained hands. He shrugged, lifting his big hands. "I want to do better."

Faith nodded. "Me too." She fingered the cash and handed him the envelope. "I added some to it. A gift from a Mr. Reynolds." She pulled out a black wallet from her pocket. She gave a small laugh.

Denny reached out and touched the freckles on her wrist.

"That spooky behavior you mentioned, it's called the uncertainty principle. The basic idea is that you can't know for certain something will happen. It's only a set of probabilities. Thus the idea that particles, and I like to think time or energy, can slip through—"

"God," Faith said. "He is just like you, Denny. Exactly. It's the most amazing thing."

She scooted over against the wall. Denny lay down on the bed next to her. The city exhaled around them, constant and fluid, the traffic heavy and humming. People argued at the bus stop two buildings away, and the breeze roused a wind chime on the balcony.

He reached over and turned off the light. Faith gasped as the ceiling ignited with his work, hundreds of bright yellowy stars, the Big Dipper, the Little Dipper, the Pleiades, Andromeda, the constellations of their birth signs. Jupiter's moons, Saturn's rings. The stain now was the Hale-Bopp Comet, with magnificent trailing sparkles. The *Columbia* space shuttle zoomed over the curvature of the earth with a thought bubble: *Thank you, Edgar Moore, for our artificial gravity! Sincerely, the NASA astronauts.*

In the dark, under a child's galactic sky, Faith and Denny did not speak. The room instead was full of silence, of particles and space and spinning thoughts. In this galaxy, the light had no distance to travel. This light was new.

This Is Not an Exit

She doesn't remember, but one summer, I left her.

It was a long time ago. Early in all this. I had just failed out of grad school, and I had broken up with this bartender at work, who, when I asked if he loved me, said, Sort of. So, at twenty-eight, I sort of had no relationship, no degree, and a job serving jalapeño poppers and beer steins to frat boys. I thought things couldn't get worse, and then she called with the news.

I left her sleeping, all alone in the house. I left in the dark, like a fugitive. Headed north, to the woods. I took her car. She wasn't supposed to drive anyway.

That cabin. Cheap, but no electricity, broken windows, about as clean as a bus station bathroom. That first night, I barricaded the door and woke up every hour on the hour, listening to the thuds and creaks, the wind gusting in the pines. At one point I heard a thin wail that sounded like a lost baby in an old dream. I tossed around on the little daybed, the smells of rottenness all around me. I remember thinking, Serves me right for leaving her that way.

In the morning, I went down the road to pick up cleaning supplies and a lantern. I bagged up beer cans, clumps of lint, beetle carcasses, a decomposed field mouse, something that looked like a human liver. I couldn't even look at the toilet yet and had to squat out by the car. By midmorning, though, the wood floors gleamed with sunshine and lemon oil. If nothing else, I could clean a house. Fix things. I got good at this as a kid when I stayed with her. I didn't have much else to do those days. I knew something about being left alone, too.

Out on the porch, I breathed in the mountain air, there in the shadow of the San Francisco Peaks, ringed by piñons and oaks. Twenty degrees cooler than in Phoenix, two dirt-road miles from the store, a cell phone with an iffy signal. Two weeks away. From her.

I walked down the porch steps with my millionth trash bag, and at the bottom I nearly stepped in a pile of scat. In the dust were paw prints as big as my hand. I didn't know much about animal tracks, but I knew enough about mountain lions from the news: during droughts, they had been known to turn dangerous, to stalk and attack humans. We were in a drought that summer. My stomach twisted. I remember I pressed my hand in the imprint, dug my knuckles into the soft dirt.

And just like that, or at least it seems to me now, things took a turn. The sound of an engine on the dirt road. A cab, black with lime-green letters across the hood. And there she was. Inside the cab, riding shotgun.

She rolled down the window and said, "Hello, dear. I see you're still alive."

I tugged at the locked door. "What's going on? Are you all right?"

The driver, a young man with a shaved head, held up a sheet of paper. My "In Case of Emergency" sheet. He said, "We GPS'd you!"

I asked, "Where's the nurse?"

She snorted the way she did, like, Nurse—ha. She pointed at

the driver and said, "We've been listening to death metal music." She laughed. She had pink lipstick on her front teeth.

The driver said, "Like you say, Miss Carol, it's no Brahms."

She said, "But we're expanding our horizons."

"Mom!" I yelled.

She looked at me. "What? I'm right here."

I never knew how she'd be from one day to the next. One hour to the next. She was only sixty-six then, but it had come on fast. The doctors said she could live in this state for a decade or more, leaking memory and reason like water from a cracked sink pipe. They were right. I was twenty-eight that summer. I'm thirty-seven now. She just had her seventy-fifth birthday, though of course she had no idea. We had cake. Marble with vanilla frosting.

The driver pushed a button on his meter. Almost $400 for that little two-and-a-half-hour cab ride.

She said, "Oh, dear."

The driver popped the trunk. "I take credit cards."

I said, "Of *course* you do."

My card was maxed with bills, so I got out hers. She stood next to the cab with a leather suitcase that was almost as big as she was.

I snatched the card and receipt from the driver. He stopped grinning and rubbed his scalp. "She said the nurse didn't show up this morning. That someone tried to break in. She seemed pretty scared when he got there, just so you know."

"No one tried to break in." I sighed and tipped him with the last cash I had. I watched as he pulled away, the cab bouncing over the ruts, dust pluming under the chassis.

She let her gigantic bag tip over into the dirt. I remember she had on her favorite blue linen pantsuit. The top bagged now, the matching pants rumpled and twisted on her hips. Her blue eyes seemed more hazel, red-rimmed, milky. She looked smaller. Not the woman I knew growing up, the one who wore suits and French twists, hurrying out the door in pointy patent leather pumps, a leather briefcase strap denting her shoulder. This wasn't her. The shape, the size, the moth-winged smell of her—all wrong.

I nodded at the cabin. "I just need to close up and then we can go home."

She said, "I thought this was your home now."

"No, only for a couple of weeks. Just vacation. Remember?"

She scrunched up her nose the way she did. "You smell like turpentine. Have you been huffing fumes?"

I stared at her.

"It's all over the news."

I said, "Mom, I failed out of grad school. I'm not a drug addict."

She said, "Well, nothing would surprise me at this point."

I didn't tell her that I had quit my "job"—she liked to put air quotes around it, as if waiting tables was another bad joke in my bad joke of a life. I'd gone to grad school because she offered to help with tuition. She told me I was a good writer. *Do something with that, Stella. Do* something.

I am trying to do something. At the very least, I'm trying to get this story down.

I told her, "I hated school, and Derrida's an asshole, but no, I am not huffing fumes. Okay?"

She waved her hand and smiled. The lipstick smudge shone on her teeth. "I could use a vacation. Work's been crazy. I've been running, running, running."

I wasn't supposed to correct or to reason with her. I was supposed to nod and agree, speaking in a patient and even tone, but I can't always help myself.

I said, "You're *retired*, Mom."

She narrowed her eyes. "You know nothing about my life."

She got me there. Of course I didn't—she hadn't been around to know. Now it had gotten more complicated: even that elusive sense of her was slipping, leaving me with, what? I didn't know. Even that word was turning on me: Know. No.

"I'm staying," she said. She picked up her suitcase and dragged it through the dirt, her bent torso aimed at the cabin like a missile.

*

We drove the two miles to the local store for supplies. She stayed quiet, looking out the window, where pine trees flashed past like an old book animation, flip, flip, flip.

"Where are we?"

"Flagstaff."

"I've never been here."

I couldn't stop the snap again. "You came up for work all the time. Your department had an office. You had a season ski pass, for Christ's sake." I punched myself in the leg for saying it.

This time, though, she laughed, her eyebrows jumping up. She touched the edges of her hair.

The store was a pull-off for travelers on their way to the Grand Canyon. I remember gas pumps, a market and diner, RV hookups. That summer day it swarmed with cars and families. Kids crowded the slushie machine and magazine racks. She tensed up at all that youthful chaos. She wasn't a "child person," as she put it, again in air quotes. *That* I have always known about her. The owner, a woman with two long gray braids whom I'd met that morning, called out hello from behind the counter. I waved but hesitated to introduce her: This is my mother. Sort of.

I loaded our cart with hundreds of dollars of camping gear, food, and more cleaning supplies. I got out her card again.

She poked my arm and launched into one of what I have come to call her Public Displays.

"Doctor Bryson and I have sex now. *Great* sex. I didn't know it could be like that." She sighed and rubbed her arms. "Certainly not with your father."

I thrust her credit card at the smirking teen cashier. "She's not well." I lowered my voice and said, "Mom."

She said, "Oh, don't be such a prude, Stella. Just because you don't have sex doesn't mean the rest of us can't be happy."

The cashier kept his eyes on the register. I signed the slip, ready to crawl under the slushie machine, but she waltzed regally out the entrance side of the doors, almost plowing down a tourist family, who stumbled to get out of her way.

*

Back at the cabin, she helped me clean. "I taught teachers how to teach. I think I can handle this," she said. She snapped on yellow rubber gloves and started spraying cleaner on the windows while I tackled the revolting bathroom. Why is it that the image of that black-ringed toilet stays after all these years? I gagged as I doused it and the moldy shower tile with bleach and Ajax, coughing at the fumes. After scrubbing awhile, I stepped back and felt a bit of pride over that salvaged white porcelain. I could fix it.

I'd learned this early, when I was fourteen, aka The Divorce Year. I moved to San Antonio with Dad, Marie, and little Cam but came back to Phoenix to live with her in the summers. She traveled most of the week around Arizona to lead education seminars, leaving me envelopes of cash and checks—plenty, she said, for food and shopping with my little friends. By then, I didn't have friends in Arizona—as if middle schoolers had time for pen pals. So I stayed home, floating in the pool or roaming the neighborhoods on my ten-speed. My first fix: the vacuum cleaner. With Dad's leftover tools, I found the busted belt and rode down to the hardware store. From there it was a dishwasher coil, a squeaking bathroom door, a loose kitchen cabinet. I bought tools and how-to books, hauled them back on my handlebars. She checked in from Kingman, Gila Bend, Sierra Vista, her voice thinner on the line. Dad called every couple of weeks, Cam screaming in the background. I would lie in bed and listen to the clicks and moans of the empty house, straining to hear the garage door, that reassuring hum. Mom was home. I'd pretend to be asleep and wait for her to lean over my bed. Sometimes she'd climb in next to me, flip our pillows to the cool side. In the morning, the sheets would still smell of her perfume. I would hold her pillow to my face. Half dreaming, I would reimagine my life. First, of course, I gave myself boobs and straight hair instead of the frizz-fest that I got from Dad. I added a wisecracking best friend who would ride bikes with me to Big Surf or come over to tan out in the backyard, where we'd pluck lemons from the tree to squeeze into our hair. I gently erased Marie but kept Dad and Cam. I gave Mom a job at the local school district, where she baked things like cobblers and blondies for weekly meetings. We'd have pizza most nights on plates that she'd make at her weekly ceramics class. Later, alone in a house where the tiles echoed, I regrouted the kitchen floor. Replaced the shower diverter. Cleaned every inch of the bath and kitchen with a rag and toothbrush until they shone like charm bracelets.

At the cabin I came out of the bathroom to find her staring out the smudged window. I picked up the paper towels and cleaner from the ledge.

She grabbed my wrist. "I'm using that."

"I was going to help." I yanked my arm away.

"That's not what you're doing. Stop treating me like a child. I changed your dirty diapers. I put you through college, for all the good it did me."

Before I could stop myself, I said, "Yes, you were the exemplar of motherhood."

She said, "Stop feeling sorry for yourself. You're too old for this sort of thing. All alone, in the middle of nowhere. What in the world do you think you're doing with your life?"

I said, "Getting away." I don't think I said, *from you*, but my meaning was clear.

She nodded. "So this is punishment. You're punishing me."

"No." But maybe I was. After all, how many times had she left me alone? I said, "This is my life, too."

She said, "Such as it is."

My life. I still dreamed then, in half-waking states, not of what I'd change but of what might happen. Sometimes this took shape as an adobe house filled with bookcases, sippy cups and animal crackers on the countertops, and an accountant who, when asked if he loved me, said, *My dear, you are the plus or minus to my margin of error.* Other times it was a loft with hardwoods and a purple lounge chair. In between there were Mexican beach houses, Italian seaside resorts, Parisian apartments, Tokyo high-rises, old cabins in the woods. I know these dreams were silly and romantic, but it was the *unknown* that hovered at the edge of my eyes, beckoning like a flickering candle in a dark attic window. Now that unknown was disappearing, slipping bright and silver down the drain before I could catch the edge of it.

She spritzed the window and ran a finger through the mist. The rubber gloves squeaked on the glass. She said, "I'm getting away, too. Away, away, away." She flitted her yellow-gloved fingers.

Something about that gesture, its light mocking, enraged me. I said, "What have you ever done but get away? From me, from Dad." I still remember the sting of bleach in my nose. I said, "You never gave up your goddamn life, and you were the mother."

She sprayed the cleaner in quick bursts until foam ran down the wall. "Is that what mothers are supposed to do? Give up their lives?"

"How would I know? I wouldn't know."

She peeled off the rubber gloves. A red rash ringed the bones of her wrist. I reached out to take her arm to examine the skin, but she crossed her arms, hiding them inside the folds of her shirt.

*

For the rest of the day, she sat on the porch and wouldn't speak to me. She barely picked at her dinner. That night she fell asleep on the daybed. I set up the new cot next to the bed and zipped myself into the new sleeping bag. The room smelled of lemon cleaner and pine and bleach. I was exhausted, but I couldn't fall asleep. Her breathing was deep and raspy. The moon lit up the room, almost bright enough to read by. I watched her chest rise and fall.

I sat up, took her purse from the side of the bed, and dumped the contents into my lap. I held objects up into the moonlight. Clorets. "Pale Autumn" lipstick. A compact with powder and mirror. In a wallet, five one-hundred-dollar bills—I had to laugh, thinking of the cab—and a picture of me around age six on a swing set, my legs stuck out stiffly. I took the cash and stuck it in my shoe. A miniature spritzer. I squirted it on my wrist, though of course I already knew the scent. I put the purse back. I sniffed my wrists. I grabbed my pillow and hugged it to my chest.

Something moved outside the front door. Rustling, a thump. I crept to the door and peered out. A raccoon dug in one of the trash bags. I stepped out and clapped at it. It didn't look at me, just kept digging. I slapped the railing, saying, "Get, get!" in a loud whisper. It finally scuttled off into the darkness. I scanned the edge of the forest. The trees' shadows were in motion, but I couldn't make out any exact shapes.

*

When I came back inside, she was sitting up.

"Where'd you go? I thought you left me."

I sat on the edge of the bed. I picked up her hand and smoothed the fingernails. "Where were you?"

"When?"

"All those years."

She pulled her hand away. "Do you remember the time I took you to summer camp up in Prescott? You glued yourself to me, and I had to drag you to your cabin. You always were so stubborn." She laughed, rocking herself a bit.

I had never been to summer camp, but I said, "I remember."

The wind gusted, and the cabin's beams creaked. Something scratched the window, a branch perhaps. She peered through the dark. "What was that?"

"It's nothing. Don't worry."

She said, "I do know you. I do."

Know. No. I remember that I pinched the insides of my elbows until my eyes burned.

She patted my arm and lay back down. She turned on her side and flipped the pillow. She said, "I like the cool side."

"Me, too." I picked up my pillow and held it to my face.

*

When I woke the next morning, she was not in the bed. I called out. No answer. I hurried outside. She was not on the deck. She was not in the car.

I started to call for her. "Mom!" I yelled. After my voice echoed to me, I stopped and switched gears. "Carol! Carol, where are you?"

After ten minutes, I spun myself in a panicked circle. I stopped and listened hard: Was that a rustle, a growl, a scream? Thin clouds covered the sky like netting. Wrong. All of it, wrong. "Help," I called out. "Someone help."

I climbed to the roof of the car and held my phone to the sky. No service. Drive, I thought. I left a note in the crack of the cabin door: CAROL: WAIT HERE.

I drove with the cell phone flipped open, watching for a signal. When I reached the store, I ran inside and asked for the phone. The teen cashier stared at me wide-eyed. He said, "She was trying to call you." He pointed to one of the aisles. "Over there."

And there she was: lying down on the concrete floor, taking a little snooze next to the charcoal briquettes and lighter fluid. She had pine needles in her hair. Her perfect hair, all ratted and poofed. A streak of dirt ran from her right temple to her lip. Scratches on her arms. A hole in the knee of her favorite blue pants.

I leaned down and shook her shoulder. "Mom. Mama. Wake up."

She bolted upright. "Don't touch me."

I said, "Mom, it's me."

She blinked in my face and scrambled to her feet. She yelled, "Get away from me!" and ran down the aisle. She ran through a doorway marked This Is Not An Exit.

The owner put a hand on my shoulder. "That's the storeroom."

People were looking in the windows. I said, "I'm so sorry."

"Please, no. Sweetheart. What can I do?"

I shook my head. I didn't know what to do. I wasn't sure I ever would know. And I was right.

I opened the storeroom door. She sat on a milk crate under a single fluorescent bulb. The string from the bulb dangled in her hair. A twig stuck sideways from her temple like a horn.

She said, "I went for a walk." She dug her palms into her thighs. "I was looking for something, but I can't remember what."

I bent low to examine the scrape on her knee, which was matted with dirt and pebbles. I held out my hand. "Will you come with me?"

She ignored my hand but got up, dusted off her pants, and walked toward the car. The owner had shooed the gawkers away, so we had a clean getaway. In the car, I pulled out the first-aid kit. She sat still, looking out the windscreen.

I handed her a gauze pad to put on her knee and started the car.

She said, "Where are we going?"

"Home."

Her eyes filled with tears. "What is this place?"

I pulled a pine needle from her bangs, rubbed at the dirt streak on her cheek. "It's just vacation, Mama. Don't worry."

We rode back to the cabin in silence. I stopped the car a few feet from the deck and cut the engine. I told her we had to pack up. We couldn't stay.

"I know this place," she said, staring through the windscreen at the cabin. She looked at me for a moment and sat back in the seat. "Is this your new home?"

I stared at the cabin. I envisioned sheer white drapes at the windows, burgundy throw pillows, gleaming wood. A place of dreams.

"No," I said.

She touched a scratch on her arm and inspected the blood on her fingertips. She looked up at the car's roof. And she said the strangest thing. She said, "It's terrifying. It's like the universe handed you a box of puzzle pieces and a bomb and said, 'Get to work. That will go off if you don't get it right, so be careful. Don't screw this up!' And there you are, with all these little cardboard pieces in your hands, and you're so afraid, just standing there, while the bomb ticks and ticks and the universe waits."

"Mom?"

She kept on. "But the bomb doesn't go off. Ever. Every time you snap in a piece and hold your breath, it sits there and ticks. Tick, tick, tick. Turns out it's not a bomb at all, just an old clock that *looks* like a bomb. And still the universe waits."

"I don't understand," I said. "I don't know what you mean."

She said, "Never mind."

"No, tell me, please tell me."

She patted my hand, but still she didn't answer.

It wasn't the first or last time that I would be left to wonder what she meant, but for some reason that moment more than others has stayed with me. I come back to it, over and over, in part, I think, because she was still mostly herself then, still the only mother I knew. Was it a metaphor? Was she talking about me? Was I the puzzle or the bomb?

What I have wished for these nine years—really, what I have always wished—is that she leaned over, tucked my hair behind my ear, and told me, "You're the universe."

But she didn't. She hasn't. She won't.

*

They tell me that this time it's happening. This time she will go, and so she is back home now. I moved her back from the facility last week when they assured me that this would be it. I have tried to fix this old house up these past few years, thanks to her savings. She wouldn't recognize the place. New paint, new windows, new cabinets and wood blinds, nice rugs over the tiles, plants, paintings, silk throw pillows. I turned the guest room into my study, and I actually study there. I'm back in school, finally. For nursing. I'm so old compared to everyone else. Such a late start. Maybe too late, but I'm doing it anyway.

It's October, and it has rained. I have thrown open the windows in her room. I have always loved the smell of the desert city after a rain: creosote, warm dirt, pavement. I don't know if she loves it too, but I'm going to say that she does, that it's something I remember about her. I have turned her pillows, covered her with a store-bought quilt—perhaps someday I will say that she made it. The warm afternoon sun slants through the blinds, casts a bronze heat.

This old house. The place where I have always waited for her. Who knew that my future would be right here? After that one exit north, I haven't left since. Some days the thought of what I have lost lands like a punch, steals my breath, and I have to get away from her again. Not permanently, but I will stand where she can't see me and wait for her to call out. Sometimes, though only sometimes now, I don't come. Other days, I feel no loss at all for those old dreams, that old half-shaped life. Because what I didn't understand then is that the unknown never *really* disappears. Every day has been new for us, hasn't it? I could never have imagined this version of us. And I cannot imagine what's next in my next life without her.

That summer. I don't know why I had to write about it today. It wasn't for her, was it? She won't read this, and even if she did, she wouldn't remember. What she knows now, where her mind has taken her, is beyond me, beyond any of us. Maybe I'm trying to make myself finally understand that. Maybe I'm trying to forgive myself, or I'm trying to punish her one last time. Am I trying to hold her close or let her go? I don't know. I'm certain that I got most of it wrong, because it's fading for me too, becoming a warped cardboard box of a memory. But that last moment comes back, fresh as today's rain: the puzzle, the bomb, the universe. No answer. We sat for a long moment in silence. I gripped the steering wheel, rested my chin on it. I blinked hard at the bug carcasses on the windshield. Finally, she opened the door and started to step out. Something moved near the deck, only a few yards from us. "Wait," I said. I grabbed her elbow, leaned over her, and shut the door with a quiet click.

At the sound of the door shutting, the mountain lion lifted its head and looked straight at us. The animal was starving: painfully thin, its spine knuckling out of the matted blonde fur, the ribs in sharp relief. It stared at the car, but then it dropped its head to sniff the ground. We watched as it climbed the steps to the cabin's door and paced a moment on the porch. It looked less like a wild animal than a lost child, confused, waiting for someone to open the door and let it in. We watched as it left the porch and cased the perimeter of the cabin, as it sniffed, peed, left scat in the dirt. We watched as, finally, it wandered toward the edge of the trees. I kept my hand on her elbow. We sat there for I don't know how long, waiting to see if it would turn back, waiting to see what it would do. But it never even looked back as it disappeared into the shadows of the pines. It never made a sound.

CPSIA information can be obtained
at www.ICGtesting.com
Printed in the USA
FFOW02n1649070715
14899FF